SEPARATED BY THE CROSS

Created and Written by:
Frank J. DeLeo

Dated August 22, 2007

Copyright © 2008 by Frank J. DeLeo

Separated by the Cross
by Frank J. DeLeo

Printed in the United States of America

ISBN 978-1-60477-613-3

Unless otherwise indicated, Bible quotations are taken from the New King James Version of the Bible. Copyright © 1979, 1980, 1982 by Thomas Nelson, Inc.

www.xulonpress.com

Craig

May God Bless

You

Thank you for your

friendship and your

support every week

Blessings!

Frank

Acts 2:21

DEDICATION

✞

This book is dedicated to my family, whom with their encouragement and love has allowed me the opportunity to go on this journey.

To my wife, Dawn, for your guidance and love that is always right on time. You truly are the LOML.

To my sons, Jon, Michael, Steven and Thomas, whom I love more than my own life. Thank you for your encouragement.

Finally to my father, John DeLeo, who has been the anchor in my life. I can't tell you how much I have gained from your wisdom and love. You are truly an inspiration.

ACKNOWLEDGEMENTS

✝

This book started out as an idea that was formed as I prepared to lead our Bible study home group one evening. I was preparing for our study and wanted to learn more about the Jewish Passover and how it related to the Christian holiday of Easter. From that study, this book was "divinely inspired." I have seen blessings of our home group with inspiration and commitment that has carried each of us through some tough and wonderful times. I will tell you that each of you have given me so much more than you could have ever known, both spiritually as well as emotionally. Blessed am I to have friends around me like these. Thank you!

Henry and Lynn Cole, Brian and Mindy Mathis, Jerry and Suzie Drew, Joe and Ana Hernandez and James and Sandy Curran: You are my brothers and sisters in Christ. Let's eat (inside joke)!

Andy McQuitty - Pastor of Irving Bible Church (IBC): For your inspiration and for opening the Scriptures in a way that I have never known. You truly are a great Pastor and leader to the community.

Cynthia Butler - A friend to both Dawn and me: For your unwavering love and prayers in getting us to IBC and ultimately leading me back to the Lord. God has blessed me with your friendship.

Becky Turner: My financial advisor and friend who told me I could do this book. I only hope it will be as successful as yours!

Cathy Payne Drewry - Editor of this book: Thank you for your help in getting this done so quickly. Your help is greatly appreciated. Thank you for your patience and understanding of my poor use of the English language.

Lynn Cole - Who was also a contributing Editor of this book: God knows I needed two Editors on this project.

Dawn DeLeo – Who helped with the editing and continually asked me, "Are you sure that's what you want to say?"

Finally, to all those who have prayed for me or believed in what I am doing, thank you: I cannot tell you the power of that type of healing. God sends angels to those who need His love to guide them along. I have been blessed to have many people who came into my life to help me—some for a reason, some for a season, and some for a lifetime. Some have been listed here, but there are many others to numerous to mention here. Each of you are special—not because of what you do, but because of who you are.

TABLE OF CONTENTS

✝

✝

"If anyone desires to come after Me, let him deny himself, and take up his cross daily, and follow Me. For whoever desires to save his life will lose it, but whoever loses his life for My sake will save it. For what profit is it to a man if he gains the whole world, and is himself destroyed or lost? For whoever is ashamed of Me and My words, of him the Son of Man will be ashamed when He comes in His own glory, and in His Father's, and of the holy angels. But I tell you truly, there are some standing here who shall not taste death till they see the Kingdom of God." (LUKE 9:23-27) NKJV

"The Spirit of the Lord is upon Me,
Because He has anointed Me
To preach the gospel to the poor;
He has sent Me to heal the brokenhearted,
To proclaim liberty to the captives
And recovery of sight to the blind,
To set at liberty those who are oppressed;
*To proclaim the acceptable year of the Lord."**

Then He closed the book and gave it back to the attendant and sat down, and the eyes of all who were in the synagogue were fixed on Him. And He began to say to them,

"Today this Scripture is fulfilled in your hearing."
(LUKE 4:18-21) NKJV

*(Isaiah 61:1, 2) NKJV

FOREWORD

✝

Try to imagine living in a time when your whole future was determined from the day of your birth—when you did not have a choice in your career path, where you would live or even who you would marry. What if you were a young man of thirteen who dreamed of being a Pharisee, one of the elite whom everyone admired, but your father insisted you follow in the family trade? You would think not much hope existed.

Many of the things people believed or studied were stories from history. All a young man of thirteen could do was to study a trade—usually the trade of his father—and hope for the best. For a woman, the hope would be that her father would have a good dowry, and if her family possessed a good trade, that would invite some wealthy person from the area to marry her. In those days, an individual's world consisted of their family, a few neighbors and friends from their village. The majority of the things learned or done were based on the laws of Moses and the traditions of the people. Thus, when a young boy journeys to Jerusalem for the Passover and sees things differently than the rest of his family, he is placed at odds with them. Doing anything other than what you were told to do was disrespectful, and breaking

away from family values or beliefs was viewed as an unfor-
givable sin to be dealt with harshly. People would be alienated from their family and, in some cases, they were never
allowed back in their town. So, when a family encounters all
this talk of the Messiah, the easy choice would be to follow
what has been set down in the law. Here is an example of
what it might be like in today's world to experience what
happened to this family two-thousand years ago.

Have you ever been to a party where everyone was
drinking, smoking, or doing drugs? You have never seen the
importance of doing such things, so when you are asked to
join in you say, "No!" Then people start excluding you from
their conversations, and they begin talking about you. What
makes it worse is they sit in front of you and laugh at you
while you watch. You want to crawl under a table and hide.
You want to fit in, and you know that doing what they are
doing will make you an instant part of the crowd, but you
know deep down in your heart this is not what you want to
do. Even though all the pressure is on you, you just cannot
give in. So you leave, alone and isolated.

In the first century, the choices made on the frontier of
following the law or following this man named Jesus Christ
were critical to individuals as well as their families. It meant
that people would be giving up everything for which they
had ever dreamed or worked. Now, compound that with the
fact that this decision was being made by a young man of
thirteen. Clearly the choice was difficult.

Have you ever had to make a decision and the fear of
making that decision appeared so critical, so overwhelming,
that you did not know what to do? How would you handle it?
What would you do? If faced with the thought of having to
give up everything, including your family, for this one decision, would you do it? Could you do it?

This is what it must have been like for fellow believers
back two-thousand years ago. They wanted to fit in and the

pressure from their families was great, but they knew in their hearts that they must follow Jesus Christ.

This story is about such decisions An entire family is turned upside down by this young man's decision and attempts to change the world and see things outside the sphere of his influence Life for this family would never be the same again.

The author hopes you enjoy *Separated by the Cross*. This fictional writing wants you to see things as they happened in the time of Jesus Christ as he dwelled among the people. The decision to follow Him is not an easy one, but then again, change never is.

DAY ONE

✟

The anticipation of the Passover was in the air and everyone, family and friends alike, were coming from all over the area. Some were coming from so far away that it took a week's journey, others just a day or so, but that did not matter. Everyone was filled with the anticipation of the Passover ritual. The streets were filled with patrons, and each merchant was excited since this was the busiest time of the year.

Dovid (David) Bar Koppel and his wife Batel (daughter of God), along with their daughter Eidel (delicate) and their son Levi (lion), were on their way to the city of David for the Passover holiday. Dovid and Batel were still in their early thirties, Eidel was nine, and Levi was thirteen—almost a man. They lived in the town called Scythopolis, a village just to the east of Mount Tabor. The area had a mixture of Romans, Jews and Gentiles. Scythopolis was a famous town in the Decopolis region. It was known as the city in which King Saul and his three sons, after being beheaded, were hung on the walls of the city for all to see. The village of Scythopolis, whose name means "house of ease," was anything but that for the Bar Koppel family. This village was a large area, heavy with agricultural farming with rich soil and occupied by the Romans. These conditions created hard times for Dovid and his family. Being a potter, his income was limited, and although they had some land, most of what they grew was for the family's consumption. Because the area was occupied by the Romans, having their personal crops stolen by the soldiers was not uncommon. Dovid and his family were accustomed to hard work. He came from a long line of potters, but he wanted more for his own son and daughter.

Dovid believed that God would provide for them in the good times as well as the bad. Dovid and Batel both had a very strong belief in God and trusted that He would guide them. They were praying daily for His coming to free all the people. At this time during the Passover feast, many people would make the pilgrimage to the city. In order to avoid problems, most families would travel in groups. Eidel and Levi would have time to play with friends and family they had not seen in a while. The adults would also talk and discuss what had happened since the last time they had gathered.

This year a buzz was present among the people; stories had been stirring about a man named Jesus who had done some amazing things. Some people were saying that He might be the Christ, while others were saying He was just crazy. Either way made for good conversation. Batel was telling her friends that she was hoping to hear and see this man who had fed five thousand people with two fish and five loaves of bread. The family was poor, and the economy was weak, so finding a place to stay was difficult. Most likely, they would stay outside the city in the tent areas. This was a common issue for most of the people who had traveled to Jerusalem. With few inns, and with almost two hundred and fifty thousand-plus people expected, surely the city would be busy.

Again, occupation of the Romans was apparent in Jerusalem as well. During the high holidays, finding Roman soldiers keeping the peace on top of the building was very common. Pontius Pilate was the governor during this time and ruled the city, causing the people to be fearful of him. The procurator was devoted to the emperor and was directly responsible to him. His primary responsibility was financial. The authority of the Roman procurators varied according to the appointment of the emperor. Pilate was a procurator *cum porestate* (one who possessed civil, military, and criminal jurisdiction). The procurator of Judea was somehow under the authority of the legate of Syria. Under the rule of a procurator *cum porestate*, such as Pontius Pilate, the Jews were allowed as much self-government as possible under imperial authority.

The Jewish judicial system was run by the Sanhedrin and court met in the "hall of hewn stone." If they desired to inflict the death penalty, the sentence had to be given and executed by the Roman procurator. Pilate made an immediate impression upon the Jews when he moved his army headquarters from Caesarea to Jerusalem. They marched into the city with their Roman standards bearing the image of the "divine emperor" and set up their headquarters right in the corner of the Temple in a fortress called "Antonia." This outraged the Jews. Pilate learned their zealous nature, along with their power within the province, and ordered the standards to be returned to Caesarea. The many crucifixions made him a very dangerous man, capable of anything.

The people had been seeking a sign from God, and as the holiday drew near, their hopes were high that maybe this year God would bless them once again with a strong harvest and plenty of work. During the trip, the women would prepare the supper as the men set up camp for the night. After their chores were done, the children would play games and listen to the stories from the old days. Electricity was in the air, and all were looking forward to the journey and arriving in the city to begin the Feast.

They had been on this route before, but this year would be different. In fact, what they were about see and hear would change everything they had ever seen or believed. Dovid announced they would leave on Tuesday and arrive on Friday evening, just before the Sabbath began, a week before the holiday. With it being so difficult to find a place to stay, leaving a few days early made it easier to get there and enjoy the week before and use this time to shop and obtain things that would sustain them the entire year.

The four-day event would be a challenge. The hike over Mount Tabor would be cold and difficult, but God would see them through. This year Levi was more excited than ever before, perhaps because he had a better understanding of the Passover or maybe because he was prepared to read the Torah during the Sabbath. Eidel was excited about this year because she would be allowed to help with preparing the meal their family would eat. When the family made camp the first night, they met up with many people whom they had not seen in quite some time. After supper the men went off and sat and talked about what was new in their businesses and families. Quite a bit of serious talk occurred among the men and the sound of the children playing around them distracted them at times. Some of the men in the group had traveled to Jerusalem a few times during the year, so many of them had heard about Jesus. They knew him as the son of the carpenter from Nazareth. Others were hearing about him for the first time.

Dovid was one of these. He paid particular attention to the elders who were wise and knowledgeable. As the men finished their prayer time and the stories drew to a conclusion, it was time to retire. Dovid, however, was intrigued by the conversations that had taken place earlier that evening. Could these stories be true? Could a mere man really restore sight to the blind, feed the multitudes, or turn water into wine? This was crazy talk; nonetheless, Dovid pondered the possibility of its authenticity, but that would have to wait for another day because he was tired. The long day took its toll on everyone.

Tomorrow would come quickly, and they had to get on the road soon thereafter. So, Dovid and his family decided to retire, but not before Levi asked his father a question: "Father, what does the Torah say about the Messiah, and how will we know when He has come?" Dovid, besides being too tired to respond, really did not know, so he told Levi that he would know when the Messiah arrives because the Messiah would rescue them from this captivity and restore their lives to glory once again. He added that they could only pray for this, and maybe someday soon, He would come and they would be jubilant.

DAY TWO

✝

As the family awoke on Wednesday morning, the air was crisp and the sky was so blue that looking at it was difficult. The brightness was blinding, and the smell of fresh fish cooking was hard to overlook. Dovid commented that he could hardly remember a better day than this. Besides the glorious weather and the smell of breakfast, a long journey lay ahead of them and he was glad the weather had cooperated. This meant they might get a little further this day and get close enough that they would be in the city by mid-day on Friday. Batel announced that breakfast was ready, and the children were already awake and ready to eat. Once breakfast was finished they would have to put things away and get on the road. Levi and Eidel knew that meant that they had better eat quickly, because there was not much time to waste.

After breakfast was eaten, they packed quickly. Eidel and Levi packed the blankets and put all the cups and mats in their places on the donkey. They once again, got on the road to Jerusalem. Since it was a long distance, Dovid tried to involve the children in a game of "can you name that plant, animal, or tree along the way?" He would point out a specimen and ask them to raise their hands and identify it. The winner would be allowed to stay up a little late that evening with papa and listen to stories and tales from the days of Moses. Levi was a good brother because sometimes he would know the answer to the questions and purposefully give a wrong answer so that Eidel could get them right. Dovid noticed this and smiled at Levi, indicating that he knew what Levi was doing. That made Dovid and Batel very proud. Along the way they would sing songs, mostly Psalms from King David and Moses. They were really enjoying their time together, making the pilgrimage easier and making the time pass more quickly.

The traveling was difficult because of the terrain and the mid-day heat. Water was sparse, so they made sure they only took little sips. They knew that the next location for water was almost fifteen miles away which was far. Since they traveled in groups to avoid trouble along the way by thieves and murderers, this route frequently took longer because they had to go inland instead of along the Jordan River.

Dovid anticipated that they would make better time because of the weather; however, what he did not anticipate was the heat. The day was unusually hot, and that meant the animals needed to stop and rest. When they got to the first stop, they stayed longer than they anticipated because the animals were hot and tired as were the people. Levi inquired of his father, "Will stopping this long delay our time in getting to Jerusalem? Will this mean we will arrive later and not on schedule?" Dovid answered him as honestly as possible and said, "The time is in God's timing—not ours, so we might be a little late, but no worries. Let us leave it up to God." Levi smiled and finished putting away the cups from the drinking water as they readied themselves to move ahead.

Aside from this being the Passover Holiday pilgrimage, it was also an opportunity for the entire family to spend a lot of time together. This was particularly exciting for Levi. Between chores and learning his lessons, he did not normally have much time to spend with his father. So he took advantage of their time together and started asking questions and telling him of things that were on his mind. However, the heat and the long travel time made Dovid irritable and short with his son. This trip was not easy on any of them. When Levi asked how much further, Dovid snapped back at him. His impatience brought a quick response from Batel. Dovid knew exactly what that meant, so he turned to Levi and said, "I am sorry my son. Please ask me what it is you want to know." They had been on the road for almost nine hours, and the entire entourage was growing weary. Their feet were sore, they were suffering heat strokes, and the animals were in need of rest. Though trees lined their way, the distance in between was too far to provide enough shade. Unfortunately, the next stop where they would stay the night would not be for almost an hour.

The family made camp just about a little over a day's journey from the final stop in Jerusalem. Upon arriving at this resting spot, they could barely make out the hillside of the Mount of Olives in the distance. Just beyond would be the City of David, but that would come on Friday. For now, they needed to get settled for the night and the hour was growing late. The men began to set up camp, including Levi and the other boys, each with his own family. The women started preparation for the evening meal. Eidel helped her mother get things started. Once dinner was finished the men went aside for evening prayers and discussed the days ahead. Some were saying that the Romans were getting worse. Aside from the pilferage they were being less responsive to the people's wishes. In fact, some were saying that the Messiah was needed now more than ever. Some said that this was even worse than when the forefathers were captive in Egypt. Dovid told the group that he believed that the time of the Messiah was yet to come, that the times were not so bad, but that they could be better. He questioned them asking how and why He would come now. The elders said He might come in a cloud with a thunderous voice and kill all the Roman soldiers, allowing them to be totally free. Others thought He would talk to the people from a cloud like he did with Moses.

Levi heard them and prayed silently to himself a Passover Psalm which would be recited every evening after the Passover meal. Levi was hoping that he would finish his studies and would be chosen to be part of a very select group of young men to follow in the Rabbi's footsteps. You see, Levi was studying diligently to achieve his goal of becoming a Pharisee. He was studying under a Rabbi named Ishaq, whose name means laughter, and was also named after the prophet Isaiah. Each day, Levi studied painstakingly with the Rabbi to learn and recite the first five chapters of the Torah. Memorizing these five chapters alone was difficult, but to be able to tell the Rabbi what chapter and verse a single word was taken from was a tremendous feat. Doing that required a special individual, which is why only just a few—perhaps only one—would be selected. They believed that if you could recite this and understand the Scriptures, you could advance to become one of the few elite who called themselves Pharisees. Levi desired this more than anything. He stayed up most nights, praying that God would allow him to be chosen for this great honor. Ishaq, in addition to his duties as Rabbi for their community, also mentored Levi and made it fun. Not only would he help Levi prepare, but he gave him wisdom along the way as to why things are the way they are. Ishaq himself was not a Pharisee, though he knew what it took to be one. When he was a young boy, he too wanted to be a Pharisee, but was not accepted into the program, a decision which broke his heart. Instead, he went back to Scythopolis and became the Rabbi, as well as helping his father on their farm.

Dovid could not afford to send Levi for special training. Since Ishaq was already in the village and he knew him well,

Dovid had asked if he would tutor his son and he would gladly pay him for his time. Ishaq made a joke that he did not have enough money or property to pay him for his knowledge, but because he liked Dovid and he had always been nice to him, he would do this on one condition. That condition was that Dovid would allow Ishaq to come over and be taught how to make pottery. You see, Ishaq was getting older and really was experiencing a difficult time. Since his family did most of the work on the farm, he was left free to keep his hands and mind busy. Dovid laughed and said, "I would be glad too, but I cannot promise anything. Your hands are like leather since you have used them all your life to farm. I give you no guarantees on how you will do." Ishaq laughed and said, "Good! Because beating the Scriptures into Levi's head will take every bit of leather I have." Dovid and Batel were very proud of Levi. It would be a great honor to Levi and his family if he were chosen. Their family had never produced a Rabbi or Pharisee. Dovid and Batel's families came from poor areas and did not have much. This placed a tremendous amount of pressure on Levi.

So while on this trip, he would sit and listen to the elders and hope to gain some wisdom into what they did and what they knew. Eidel was learning many things also, mostly how to prepare food, wash clothes, and how to clean. These tasks were very important because she was almost a woman and both her parents were trying to get her ready for the future. At age twelve or thirteen, she would be ready for marriage. Since the family did not have a lot to give, they were hoping that Eidel's marriage arrangements would place her in a good wealthy family from the town. If Levi were able to obtain the status of Rabbi or Pharisee, that might help Eidel's chances for a more elite status as well. So the pressure on Levi was even greater. Every night Levi would recite his memorized Scriptures of the first five books of the Torah. Then he would work on the remaining books of Scripture.

This was critical for his advancement to Bates Talmud. Once he was done practicing, Eidel came over to Levi and asked him if he wanted to find finished rocks to wash the clothes in the morning. He said, "No," and just pushed her away. He was in deep thought, desiring to help his father with the discussions on the Messiah. As a young man his eye was on completing Bates Talmud then on to achieving the next level of education, the "Midrash," which meant he was ready to follow a Rabbi. Ishaq was going to help him achieve that goal and someday become Ishaq's apprentice, but right now all he wanted to do was help his father, and by doing so that would show great maturity on his part. But, that would have to wait, because the men finished praying and said their goodnights. Again Levi walked directly behind his father, attempting to mimic his walk and his deep thoughts about what was said and how to make sense of it.

As night time approached, the area grew bitterly cold as the wind began to pick up. The terrain was very difficult as they climbed the mountainous crossing of Mount Gerizim, just to the east of Samaria and about six miles to the west of the Jordan River. The limited amount of protection from trees made it easy for the wind to come whistling through the area and blow everything and everyone around. More importantly, keeping the fire going at night presented quite a challenge. In the past, some people had wandered off, suffered snakebites, or worse yet, froze to death. Making sure to keep warm at night was critical. Only limited shelter was available out in this area. No caves existed to sneak into or to protect them from the elements. This night, they were in the direct midst of the wind and cold. Someone would be required to stay up and keep watch for animals, weather, and the fire to make sure that it did not extinguish itself. Each family suggested someone to take on this responsibility; each night two or three families were required to keep watch. Tonight, Dovid chose Levi to make the fire and keep guard for the family and the others around. He suggested Levi for several reasons; it was their family's turn, and he recognized that Levi was eager to be considered a man. Also, since earlier in the day Dovid had been short with him, this was his way of demonstrating to his son that he still had favor with his father. But more importantly, he had faith in his abilities. Levi was excited when he was told that this night he would be responsible for the fire and keeping guard of the area.

Levi and the others went out seeking kindling and other wood to make the fire for the evening. When Levi's turn to stand guard came it was at the most difficult time; 2:00 to 6:00 in the early morning. Although staying awake was hard, he took his responsibility seriously. The fire was well underway and Levi was making sure he was doing his part. One of the ways he would stay awake was to work on his memorizations of the Torah. Second, was to sit and think about how the Messiah would come. Levi was getting very cold, and even though he kept an eye on his family, he was hoping that the time would go faster and that dawn would arrive soon. He kept looking to the east for the sign of early morning daylight, but it did not arrive. Then he heard a stirring and noticed that his sister had moved closer to his mother. Moving closer allowed them to use their mutual body heat to stay warm. He was hoping his sister would arise and sit by the fire with him to keep him awake. He realized that earlier that night, he was unkind to his sister and that he needed to say he was sorry when she woke up. By now the wind was really whipping around, and he was doing everything he had been taught to keep the fire going. The one thing he did not want to happen was for it to go out. If that happened, it meant trouble for everyone. He would not only be embarrassed, but he would feel awful that he had let down his family and the entire entourage as well. Finally, the wind died down and it became very quiet. Peace reigned in the air with not a cloud in the sky. The full moon lit the sky and made all the stars in the heavens visible. As he looked up, he tried the impossible job of counting the stars. He thought to himself, how beautiful they all were and then remembered the verse about God flinging the stars into the heavens and knowing each one by name. He thought to himself, "I wonder what each of their names might be?" How could God know the names of all the stars? So many existed, how could he remember their names? Then, he heard his sister stirring again and thought that maybe she was awake and that would give him someone to talk to. She was just cold and moving to get closer to her parents. So, once again it was just him, the night air, the sound of the animals and a few people snoring to drown out his own quiet. In a way that was good, because it gave him something to keep him occupied. He tried to keep rhythm with the sounds.

His thoughts began to wander toward God and his infinite understanding of everything. He thought back to the conversation earlier that evening when all the men were discussing when the Messiah would come and how He would come. Levi began to theorize himself how it would happen. He thought the Messiah might burst from the clouds with a tremendous sound. He might not even descend from the sky at all. What if He just looked down from heaven and waved His mighty right hand and destroyed the Romans? That would be good. "I know," Levi thought, "He will strike them down with a bolt of lightning. Maybe He would do something similar to what He did when Moses was on the earth and kill the first-born, like he did during the first Passover. After all, did they not know that we are the chosen people? Did they not know that God was their Father and that they would be freed from this captivity? Maybe plagues were going to reoccur, and the Romans would realize that they needed to leave the area before worse things happened." But the thought of what the Messiah would look like and how He would come and what He would do were continually on his mind. After he listened to the stories of the man they called Jesus of Nazareth, and heard what everyone had said, he just did not know what to make of it.

People were mixed in their opinions. Some testified that they had seen people who they had known all their lives who were crippled or blind, and this man had healed them. He also remembered that others indicated that He was a blasphemer and that He was using magic to do the things He was doing. Others believed He had enlisted people to fake their infirmities to make Him look good. How would they know the difference? What signs would be present? He thought about what he had learned in his studies from the old text that Isaiah had foretold of one who would come and save the world, or that of the prophet Daniel who told that He would come and save people from their sins. Even King David foretold of one who would take mankind's place and would be pierced for their transgressions. How would He come and when would He come? Levi thought to himself that our people have been waiting a long time and wondered how much longer they would have to wait. The thought of it all was making his head hurt. It was very difficult to understand, and the harder he tried, the more confused he became.

As he lay looking up at the stars, he could not help but wonder which star was heaven and how far away it was. As he stared upward, he kept thinking, could this man be the one? If He was able to do these things, why did anyone not really believe Him? If He was the Messiah, surely the Pharisees and the Sadducees would know Him. They were the most learned people, and they could tell between the real thing and a fake. His mind was spinning, and all this created even more confusion for him. He shut his eyes for a moment to clear his head and fell asleep. A few minutes later he felt a tap on his shoulder and opened his eyes. He saw his father's face looking at him and calling his name quietly. Levi quickly jumped to his feet and said, "I am awake. I just closed my eyes for a minute, not to worry Father." With a loving smile, his father said, "I know son. I was just thinking about you and could not sleep, so I thought I would come out and keep you company." They were trying to whisper, and the hour was only about 4:30 in the morning. Dovid told his son about the first time he was given the chance to watch over the camp and how he fell asleep for most of the night. He related how he awakened just before morning and how he rushed to get the fire going because it had basically gone out. He told Levi how he got so nervous that he caught his garment on fire trying to fan it so it would stay lit. Levi asked what happened. Dovid said the garment went up in flames, and the fire was rekindled. Levi smiled as Dovid laughed. Levi motioned to his father to be quiet so as not to awaken the others. That set them both to laughing.

Dovid could see that something had been troubling his son all night, and he asked Levi, "What is wrong? What is on your mind?" Levi began to tell his father about his concerns about the Messiah and His coming, and he was consumed by the power of what God could do and comprehend. He went on to tell his father how he was having a difficult time understanding the issues that were being raised about this man named Jesus. He described for his father the Scriptures pertaining to what the prophets foretold of His coming and that after hearing Ishaq speak of Him, he was concerned about the debate and what this would mean. Ishaq was a very knowledgeable man and Rabbi, so Levi had always trusted in his wisdom. Ishaq and others were inquiring whether this man, Jesus, could be the Messiah. How could they know for sure, and what signs would it take to be convinced? But then Levi asked that if He was truly the Messiah, since they were His people, would they know Him or not?

Dovid was amazed at his son's thinking and the rationale behind his thoughts. He was really becoming a man. Before he answered his son, he needed more information, so he asked Levi, "Why are you so concerned with this man and the things He has done? You know the Scriptures—what do they say about His coming?" Levi responded that it had been written that He would come to release mankind from captivity, that He would free them, and that He would crush the head of the serpent. More to the point, He would perform wonders and signs that would prove that He was the Messiah. So Dovid said, "Why are you worried? You know what is foretold and what He will do, and you know He will do wondrous miracles." "Yes, Father. That is the point—people are saying this man, Jesus, is the Messiah, and if He is, why do others call Him a fake?" Dovid thought for a moment and responded, "Maybe we will get a chance to see this man while we are in Jerusalem and see for ourselves whether or not He is the one." This brought a smile to Levi's face as he put his head against his father's shoulder.

As they sat facing the east, time must have slipped away, for the sun was beginning to rise. Levi was having the best time of his life. That evening had been one of the best he and his father had *ever* spent. Now, even more than before, Levi was filled with excitement to think it was the Passover holiday and a chance existed that he might see this man called Jesus. Maybe, just maybe, He *was* the Messiah. If life had ended right then, that would have been okay with Levi. He felt life could not get any better than this.

Dovid realized that this night his son truly had become a man. Levi no longer thought of childish things such as playing games or getting his sister in trouble. He was thinking about the history of his people and the possibility for the Messiah's coming. Dovid was grateful to God for his son and the blessing He had bestowed upon him. Trying to hold back his tears of joy, Dovid sniffled, and Levi looked at him and said, "Father, why are you crying?" Dovid responded, "I am not crying my son. The cold has gotten into my eyes and caused them to tear up." This was a moment that neither father nor son would ever forget.

With the sun rising, Dovid said to his son, "We had better get a move on. Everyone will be getting up soon and the women will need a bigger fire in order to cook." Although neither wanted that moment to end, they realized that chores had to be done if they were going to arrive in Jerusalem by mid-day tomorrow. Just a few minutes later, the people started to stir, and the day was upon them giving no more time for deep thinking. They had work to do.

DAY THREE

✝

Thursday was always the hardest for many reasons, but mostly because they all knew that they were more than halfway there. As in any trip, the closer to the destination, the more anxious everyone gets. A scream emitted from one of the tents, a very loud scream that woke up anyone who might still be asleep; however, one of the travelers did not wake up. Perhaps the cold had caused it or merely his age, but either way, a man had died that night. This was not an uncommon situation, as many expected to have someone lose their life on these trips. The trip was not easy, and many people got sick or were lost due to the difficult weather conditions in which many things can happen. However, when Dovid and Levi arose and ran to the tent, they were surprised to find it was the Rabbi Ishaq. How could this happen to this man? He was a very good and honest man who worked hard to help everyone, and he was such a voice of reason among the elders. This was devastating to everyone concerned, but to no one more than Levi.

Levi was upset because his mentor, his friend, and one of the elders—their Rabbi—was gone. Levi had fond memories of this gentle man. He had spent many evenings in Scythopolis at his feet learning about the Torah and what he needed to do to become a Pharisee. Levi, along with the families on the journey, was truly saddened by his death.

Since Ishaq had taken Levi under his wing, he had become a part of the Bar Koppel family. He was there most nights until late, working with Levi. Batel would ask him if he needed anything, and his answer was always the same, "Something to warm my feet." She would laugh, because that meant a little bit of wine. He would look at her and smile, and then, some evenings he would tell her how proud he was of her son and how hard he was working to achieve his goals. He would further say that Levi was getting better every day, and that before she knew it, he would be ready to assume the role of the Rabbi's assistant. Ishaq looked upon Levi as a father to a son.

With Ishaq's own sons grown and now running the family farm business, this was a chance for him to rekindle his own dreams, his own wishes for his sons. Levi had found him to be a very kind and wonderful man, recalling how much he enjoyed studying and learning on the floor of his home, while looking up and seeking assurance from his mentor. Ishaq always made the stories and learning fun and enjoyable. Dovid said that he thought Ishaq's name fit his personality very well. Everyone loved him. Just a few hours earlier he had been one of the people giving his opinion on who Jesus was and saying he felt that if God was going to send a Messiah, the time was now, and that this person fit many of the prophecies depicted in the Scriptures.

Ishaq had made the trip to the Holy City just a few weeks ago and was privileged to be at the wedding in Canaan when this man, Jesus, turned the water into wine. He told the group what he had observed. He was the voice of reason during the sessions, telling the people that he felt that this was the Messiah and that, when they got to Jerusalem, he would take them to see Him. They could see for themselves and make up their own minds as to this man's identity. Ishaq told them that finding Him would not be difficult. When He was in town, great crowds were always surrounding Him, leaving no room for mistaking who He was. Levi was always confident in his teacher. If Ishaq felt this man was the Messiah, then he must have witnessed something that convinced him. This was even harder for Levi, now since his mentor was gone.

Losing Ishaq was so devastating for Levi that all the excitement of just a few hours earlier had gone quickly. Levi was grieving and sobbing so uncontrollably that Dovid was having a difficult time just holding his son. Now his mother, Batel, and his sister, Eidel, were present also, just looking on in disbelief. Everyone who knew this man knew of his kindness and love for all people and how he made people laugh. Batel looked on and began to cry as she remembered the last time she was in the presence of the Rabbi. She thought of how he made her laugh; she recalled how it had been awhile since that had happened. He always found a way to make her feel good about herself and accentuated her importance in the family. She saw him teach her tender young son; she was present day after day as he spent time with her son, guiding and giving him an understanding of the Scriptures. He had reminded her of her own father so many years ago. She could see the bond that her son had with this man. Levi looked at him as more than a mentor; he was like a grandfather to him. Ishaq had touched her life also; yes, she was weeping because of her son's anguish, but also because she felt the loss as everyone else did. As they stayed there praying over him, she recalled just yesterday when he had spoken to her about the man, Jesus,. Most of the elder men thought he was getting old and losing his senses. Many of them played along, asking him questions to keep the old man involved, but she knew differently. She knew that he still had his faculties. He made perfect sense when he spoke; they spent only ten to fifteen minutes together, but Ishaq made everything come to life when they spoke.

In that time, two things caught her attention. First, the stories he told her of Jesus were amazing! As he spoke to her she watched his eyes. His dark eyes, which had lost their color and brightness years ago, now seemed alive, dancing like stars as he told her of this man's deeds. His skin glowed again. Over the years as he aged, his skin had begun to dry, largely due to the weather conditions, but this day his skin had glistened as if he had just taken a bath. Second, he was alive again. He had a new step about him, he was singing old forgotten hymns of long ago, and was reciting old prophecies as if they were just first heard. He looked at her with such confidence and spoke plainly to her about Jesus and how he did the things that he did. To think that the Messiah might finally have come made her excited. She believed him and, more importantly, she knew her son was learning from a very wise and gracious Rabbi. He was not only having an influence on her young son, but on her as well. How did this happen? What did he see? Could this excitement be real? Was this just an elderly gentleman getting close to the end of his life? She was looking forward to seeing Jesus together with Ishaq. She was hoping that he could introduce her. She did not know if they had ever really met or whether Ishaq had just seen Jesus from a distance.

Ishaq's death was such a shock. How could this happen now to this man and to this village? How would they be able to enjoy the Passover? As the morning progressed, and as things came to a conclusion, the family went back to the tent and began to put things away so they could move on to Jerusalem. Dovid and the others saw to Ishaq's remains, while the wives and children began to clean up. Levi, as well as Eidel, was still in shock. Eidel had never seen a dead person. The mere fact that she knew him well made it an even more traumatic experience for a nine-year-old. Ishaq's death really put things behind schedule, so much so that they most likely would not get to Jerusalem until either late Friday or would have to wait until early Sunday, fore they could not travel or work on the Sabbath. Batel knew the family must eat if they were going to make it through the end of the day. The fact that no one was hungry was obvious, but they still needed nourishment. So Batel and Eidel decided to make a small breakfast. They did this for two reasons: first, because they needed to eat, and second, because it gave them something to do to help with the grieving process. So mother and daughter prepared a light breakfast of dried fruits and nuts, along with some bread that would sustain them until later in the day.

Levi told his mother he was not hungry, but she would not hear of it. "You must keep up your strength for the journey," she said. He tried to tell her that he was not interested, but she just kept telling him that he must eat something. As they began to thank God for the food, Levi began to cry again. He was heartbroken and confused as to why God would do this now. Ishaq was a good man, teacher, and personal friend. What would happen now? More questions existed than answers. He remembered that Ishaq explained about heaven and where God is and that he is a good God and, most importantly, that God takes care of his children. Since they were his chosen people, they had nothing to fear. Now, Levi was more confused than ever. He prayed to God quietly, asking for understanding and wisdom on what had happened and why. But nothing would ever be the same again. In his mind, God was punishing him or his family, and he did not understand why. As they began to eat, Dovid came back in and sat down. Everyone could tell he was very upset. He had lost an old friend—someone he knew would have helped his son become a man. A wiser man he did not know. He took a look at Batel, and she knew that he had laid his old friend and Rabbi, Ishaq, to rest. As they began to eat, no other words were spoken; they just tried to remember the good things about their friend. Dovid was strangely affected by Ishaq's death. Previously, he had seen many men die, even members of his own family, but he could not get over how much impact Ishaq had had on the entire entourage. So many of the people were impacted by this man's life and teachings that Dovid was overwhelmed the more he thought about it. He glanced across the tent at his wife with tears in his eyes. She began to cry which started everyone crying again.

Dovid was not a very emotional individual, but for some reason, this death really affected him. He held his family close and simply stated, "Ishaq is at peace and is now with our Forefathers, Abraham, Isaac, and Jacob." As they again sat on the ground, he tried to make sense of all this. He began to recount in his mind the events of the day and what had happened. He thought of Ishaq's face when he saw the body and how he had looked. He truly was at peace. He recalled how natural he looked. He had never seen a dead person look so well. In fact, he recalled that the man's eyes were bright and staring up at heaven as if he had seen the place and was so overcome with joy that he just did not want to stay here any longer. He also remembered in the days before, when they would talk, how he looked different, and the way he spoke was electrifying. He did not think much of it then, but now it seemed odd to Dovid. Was he really changed by what he saw in Jerusalem, and could all that Ishaq said be true? He hoped for his sake that it was. He recalled over the last few days that Ishaq was sharing with everyone who would listen about what he saw and heard. How this man said things that astounded everyone! Dovid did not think much of it then. In fact, all of the elders from the village just let him ramble, but now, Dovid was trying to recall all that Ishaq had said and what it all meant. That look and the way he talked began to weigh on his mind. One thing is sure—this was like no other pilgrimage to the Holy City.

Dovid collected his thoughts and looked once again at his family. They realized they really did not want to leave, even though they needed to go. So, they finished the little they ate and cleaned up what was left. They packed up the remaining garments and materials, and would be on their way shortly. The other groups were ready to go. They had marked the spot where they had laid Ishaq to rest, and they would be back this way on the way home. They would check on things and try to make a more permanent marker upon their return. The day was almost one-third over, so they needed to get moving if any chance at all existed to make it to Jerusalem by that evening.

The closer they got to the northern side of Jerusalem, the more difficult the travel became. The incline of the hillside along with the terrain, and more rocks and debris on the roadside required them to slow down. The group realized that they would not make it to the Holy City by evening, so they would have to stop along the way. Dovid and the other men began to think about what they would do and where they should stay. Things were made even worse by the weather, which had been great so far, but was turning dark. Gray clouds were moving in and the smell of rain was in the air. Normally, Dovid liked the smell of rain off the horizon, but not today. Rain would mean even more delays—more trouble with the animals and all the provisions they had with them.

The impending rain meant they needed to find shelter. The closest shelter Dovid knew was in Sychar, just to the east of Mount Gerizim, which was at least two hours away. They needed a backup plan if they could not get there—were there any alternatives? Did anyone in the group know of any other locations along the route? Maybe one existed off the main road. He began to ask the others if they knew of any other locations. Most had the same idea as Dovid, but again the shelter was two hours away. Dovid could not help but think, "If Ishaq was here, I bet he would know exactly where to go." That got him to rethinking about his long-time friend and mentor to his son. He thought back on what his last few days were like with him. How excited Ishaq was, and how mad he had become at some people when they pushed off his idea of the Messiah being in Jerusalem. Ishaq began to shout at people to listen to him.

Dovid particularly remembered their first evening, Tuesday, when they stopped for the day. After supper the men got together for prayers and a lively discussion. Ishaq led the prayer session where he told the group about his encounter with this man, Jesus,, and how He was to change everything. The more Ishaq talked, the more the others began to think he had lost his mind. Most were skeptical of what was being said, but Ishaq kept saying to them, "What do the Scriptures say about His coming? When did you all get so powerful and mighty that you do not recognize the God of Abraham, Isaac and Jacob?" Dovid listened when they all discussed the prophecies and how they were being fulfilled. He recalled that Ishaq told the group that he personally had seen Jesus walk by a crippled man who was waiting to get into the water to be healed. He related that Jesus stopped as the man was crying for help and that Jesus asked him what he wanted. The crippled man said he wanted help to enter the water to be healed. Jesus said to him, "Stand up and pick up your bed and go home." As the crowd gathered, this man stood up and picked up his bed and walked away. He amazed the crowd, and some of the Pharisees and Priests questioned Jesus about why He would do this on the Sabbath. Ishaq explained that Jesus told the Pharisees they were hypocrites. They got angry and wanted to take action against Him, but they just walked away. When Ishaq finished telling them the story, they all were taken aback, and many asked, "How can this be?" But, Ishaq was so positive and confident that many of the group said, "We do not want to disagree, but we would have to see it ourselves."

Dovid left that evening, confused and uncertain as to whether any or all of this was possible. But, Dovid knew his friend would not lie, and he did not make up stories. Then how could this be a man healing another man? One thing was for certain, Ishaq believed it and whatever he saw changed his life forever. He was different, and more importantly, the last days of his life were filled with hope and joy. Dovid could not deny the passion and commitment that his Rabbi had over the last several weeks of his life. He had never seen anyone so committed to anything. The way he told the stories, you could actually envision yourself being present. Maybe this is why Dovid walked away that night confused. In some ways he really wanted to believe his friend, but if he did, how would that look to the other men in the village? Plenty of time lay ahead to think about what his friend saw and said, but right now, the only thing Dovid knew was that his old friend would know where they could stop for shelter, and he was not present now to help.

The weather really worsened the closer they came to Mount Grizim. The air became heavier and the humidity was so thick that you could almost see it in the air. It got darker and the lightning over the mountain in the distance grew brighter. They were still at least about forty minutes away from an area where they could stop. By now the animals were getting skittish, and the people were concerned about being caught out in this storm. One man who joined the caravan along the way told the group a place to stop existed about sixty minutes to the west. They decided that was not a good idea because they were closer to Sychar. Thus, they decided to keep walking south. As it started raining they continued to walk. As they did, their clothes were soaked from head-to-toe. The closer they got to the mountainside, the harder the rain came down. The road was terribly muddy now, making it difficult for the animals, the people, and the carts to move at a pace to get them out of the downpour. Everyone was having a difficult time seeing with the rain coming down in front of them. Some of the people stopped and said they could not go any further. They wanted to stop and cover themselves, but the others said, "No, we must continue on. We are almost there." When the lightning and the thunder hit just in front of them, the animals got frightened, and they began to try to break away. The people became terrified. Dovid and Batel were trying to keep the children covered as much as possible, but no matter what they did, it was no use. In fact, Dovid needed Levi to help him with the livestock to make sure they did not get away. The animals were very expensive, and since they did not have much money, they needed them to barter in town to get supplies.

So much water and mud were on the ground that it made it difficult for Levi, and even Dovid, to have any traction to hold the animals still. People were slipping and sliding all over, merely trying to keep themselves from falling. The puddles were getting larger, and the rain was falling so hard that it flooded the area. The harder they tried to move forward, the more mud they sank into. That last mile seemed never-ending. When they reached their destination, the cave they entered had just enough room for the people. Therefore, the animals needed to remain outside. Dovid got his family inside while he and the other men stayed outside in the pouring rain, trying to secure the animals and the carts. They tied them as best they could. Levi noticed his father was having a difficult time so he ran out to help. That just complicated things more, because Dovid, aside from trying to keep the animals secure, had to explain to Levi how to restrain them so they would not get away. It took some time, but they secured them, and got back under cover. By this time, they were so wet that they were cold, and the water had made their clothes so heavy they needed to change;

however, by now, most of what they had was wet as a well. Luckily, a few clothes in the middle of the bags were still dry. Dovid and his family took turns changing, and by now the rain had begun to let up a little. This really put them way behind schedule and at this point, there was no sense trying to make it over the mountain. They would have to spend the night in this place. All the men agreed that the weather was still too uncertain, and traveling over the mountain in this mud and rain would make it almost impossible for the group. Dovid was the first to agree with the others by saying, "I think we should just make camp, dry out what we can, feed the animals and get a fresh start in the morning." No one was happier than Levi to hear this news. He was exhausted and a little afraid of heading out again. Between the rain, lightning, and thunder, that was not something he wanted to experience again any time soon. Eidel was crying. She had never been outside in weather like this before. She was cold and wet and could not seem to get warm. Her mother, trying to keep her close, put some layers of clothes on her but the layers were useless. They were hoping to begin a fire, but any wood that could be retrieved would be wet at this point. The shelter would keep them out of the rain, but it did not really help with the cold when night fell. Dovid and the other men were very concerned about how they would keep themselves and their families warm that night.

Once the rain stopped, Dovid and the others went out to see what they could do. Unfortunately, some of the animals had gotten loose because they could not keep the ropes tied down with the mud. As Dovid went out, he noticed that two of his animals were missing. Other men were searching for their animals as well. The good news was that some of the animals that had gotten loose did not roam far; however, others did, and the men worried that they would not be able to reclaim them. The sky was still dark, and although the rain had stopped, the lightning and thunder were still loud. This time Levi did not volunteer to go out with his father to try to find the lost animals. Dovid realized that he did not have much, but if they did not find the lost goat, they would not be able to buy much. That meant that they would have to do without a lot this next year.

As Dovid looked up and to the south, he could tell that the weather had not passed yet. Heading out to look for the animals was not a good idea; however, he also realized that if he did not, they would never get their goat back. He and three other men decided their families needed those animals to survive next year, so they decided to try to find them. Dovid took Levi aside and said that he expected him to help his mother until he returned. Levi had a strange look on his face, and Dovid asked him what was wrong. Levi looked his father right in the eyes and said, "When will you be back?" Seeing the fear in Levi's eyes, Dovid replied, "Not too long. Do not worry—just look after your mother and sister until I get back. You are the man of the house while I am gone." Then Levi asked, "But why do you have to go now? Can it not wait until all the weather passes?" Dovid looked at Levi and said, "Do not worry. I will be fine. Just do what I ask; you are the man of the house right now. I expect nothing less than your best." Levi shook his head and replied with an okay. Dovid and the others headed out, and Levi returned to his mother and sister and told them not to worry, that he would take care of them until his father returned.

In his whole life, Levi had never worried about his father. He never feared for him before, and he did not like the feeling he was having. He had always seen his father as being invincible and as being the biggest and strongest man that he had ever seen. That had changed on this trip, but not because his father was not able to take care of himself. Maybe it was because, for the first time, he was old enough to understand that fathers had no control over the elements, or maybe because they had lost Ishaq. Whatever the case, Levi was frightened, and with good reason.

No sooner had they left than the weather began to start up again. This time the rain was pounding profusely and they had never seen rain like this before. All the families could do was to watch the rain which was coming down so hard that all they could see was the end of the cave. So, as hard as Levi tried to see if he could still see his father, he could not, and that made him even more concerned.

Not wanting to show signs of weakness before his mother or sister, he kept it to himself. Some of the other members of the group, on the contrary, were talking amongst themselves saying that the weather was very bad, and they were concerned about the team that went out after the animals. They feared for their lives. Levi immediately felt sick to his stomach. He did not want anything to happen to his father, and he did not care if they found the animals or not. He just wanted his father to come back. So he began to pray to God for his help. He recalled how King David fell on the ground and prayed hours on end without eating, drinking, or changing his clothes. Levi, now on the ground—hands and arms spread apart and his face buried in the dirt—prayed for deliverance, asking God to bring his father back safely. He asked God again and again to keep his father safe under his wing and not to allow him to be harmed, and he petitioned for the groups' safe return.

Batel saw her son in the corner praying quietly to himself, and she asked, "For what are you praying, my son?" He told her that it was for his father's safe return. Batel told her son that God would guide his father, that he was a good man, and that God would see him back safely. Levi looked at his mother with his eyes full of tears and said, "But Ishaq was a man of God, and God decided to take him, so maybe He will do the same with my father?" Batel really did not have an answer for her son and, more importantly, she did not want her son to see the fear in her own eyes, so she smiled and walked away before she began to cry. Levi prayed from Deuteronomy for his father: *"Only take heed to yourself, and diligently keep yourself, lest you forget the things your eyes have seen, and lest they depart from your heart all the days of your life."* Then he continued and recited David's Psalm: *"But let all those rejoice who put their trust in you. Let them ever shout for joy, because you defend them; Let those also who love your name be joyful in you. For you, O Lord, will bless the righteous; with favor your will surrounds him as with a shield."*

Levi felt that God was good. Ishaq had told him that, with God, if you fear the Lord He will bless you and your family. Levi believed that his father was a good man and feared the Lord, so God would deliver him back safely. But, even though Levi knew the Scriptures, he was scared. He prayed the prayers in hopes that his plea to God would be sufficient, but he also knew that he needed to continue to ask for God's blessing on his family and right now on his father. Batel again walked over to Levi and listened intently to her son. My, how he had grown and how well he prayed. Surely God would listen to her son who was praying for his father and for the others who were also with him. Time did not seem to move—it was as if it was standing still. Minutes began to feel like hours, and the entire entourage was now praying. The more they prayed the harder it seemed to rain and the louder the thunder became. It seemed as if God had stopped listening to them. He had turned away from them.

Batel needed to try to keep herself busy, so she returned to her daughter in an attempt to keep her occupied. Batel sang quietly to her, and as she did, she kept an eye on the entrance to the cave in hopes of seeing her husband coming in the distance. Levi was lying there reciting the prayers over and over again. He was getting frustrated because he did not understand why God had not answered his prayer yet. He feared the worst and began to think maybe his father was not coming back. The weather was not letting up and he thought that by now, he should have been back. Where could his father be? As the man of the family, he needed to stay close to his mother as he had promised his father, but maybe if he went out and searched for his father, he could find him and bring him back. He thought that if God was not going to answer his prayer, then maybe he should go out himself and rescue his father. What seemed like hours was, in actuality, only about twenty minutes. The rain began to slow again and visibility returned. He could make out the animals that were present. They were all huddled together and stuck in the mud, which at that point was a blessing because had they not been so deep in the mud, they might have all escaped. The rain and wind did not give any hope for keeping them tied down.

Levi and the entire group continued to pray for their safe return. The rain was so fierce, and with such strong winds, there was no telling where they might be or in what condition they might be found. Levi closed his eyes and asked the Lord God, "I have asked and asked, and yet you have not answered. Why? Have you turned your ear away from your servant? I follow the commandments set forth by our Forefather, Moses; I have done all that you ask and my family has as well. Why, then will you not grant me this request? I am at a loss as to what to do. You know all and are all-powerful. I ask for your blessing on my family and the group as we travel to the Holy City for the Passover. Lord, please grant me this one request, and I will do whatever you ask of me. I will give up all I have for this one request." As Levi opened his eyes they were wet from the tears, and his face had dirt—even mud—on it from lying face-down on the ground, and his tears which had fallen on the dirt had become mud. As he lifted his head and turned, visibility was skewed, but he peeked out the cave opening. He did not see anything. As he wiped his eyes he noticed that the rain had ceased. Now, they could at least go out and search for his father and the others.

Levi arose and looked at his mother and sister and said, "I will go find our father." Batel shouted at him, "No, I do not think you should go out in this weather," but Levi was determined to go anyway. Again, his mother rebuked him and reminded him of his father's request to stay with the family until he returned. He was the man of the house and, as such, his responsibility was to be with them. By now, many of the men were once more outside trying to secure the animals and hoping that none of them had been injured or washed away with the heavy flooding. As the temporary head of the household, Levi was responsible to help them. He recalled how important this was to him just a few days ago. He remembered that he was so excited when his father allowed him to be accountable for the evening fire and making sure they all were safe. But now, he did not want the job. He would gladly give it up if his father would just come back. He prayed again as he went outside, "Lord, please let me look to the west and see him and the others coming back and I will never ask to be head of the household again."

As he worked with the others, he looked to the south and noticed a rainbow in the distance, remembering God's commitment of His covenant with His people. This was a good sign; surely God would answer his prayer! He looked back into the cave and saw his mother and the other women looking out, hoping to see the men, but her face looked long and worried. Levi thought to himself that he had never seen his mother with this look of fear on her face. This was the very first time her eyes revealed what her heart feared. Batel caught a glimpse of Levi watching her, and she turned to him, smiled, and nodded at him in a feeble attempt to convince her son that everything was going to be okay. He was not convinced. In fact, this made him feel all the more concerned. What if his father did not come back? How would they survive? What would the family do? Would they become orphans? Who would take care of them, and what could he do to get work? What could he do?

On a few occasions, Levi had worked with his father with pottery, but he was not skilled like his father. His father had bigger plans for him; Levi was to study to become a Pharisee. But, that would take time, and who would care for his family in the meantime? How could God have allowed this to happen? Why would God take the only two men Levi had ever trusted and cared about, both in the same week? Was God testing him? What about his mother? She was a great woman and a devoted child of God. Why would God make her a widow now? So many questions and Levi had no answers! The more he thought, the more questions surfaced, like who would make sure his sister got married? Who would want her if no one was present to arrange the marriage? If her father was not around, how would Levi accomplish that? He had no experience with this; what was needed? Who would be a good person with whom to match her?

Levi reasoned that if his father did not return, he would not be able to continue to pursue his dream of becoming a Pharisee. He would have to go into another field, and as he tried to take his mind off all the pressure resulting from his fear and questions, he noticed that the sun was breaking through the dark clouds. In fact, the sun shone so brightly that he could hardly look out without being blinded by the sunlight. Again, he looked to the west, but still no sign of the men. By now, another hour had passed, and the men were all finished securing the animals to make sure they would not go anywhere. Levi retreated into the cave, and his emotional ups and downs were taking their toll. Levi just lost it when Eidel asked, "Should we not make a fire so we can warm ourselves?" He replied in a loud voice, "How can you worry about a fire now when our father is lost out there somewhere, and we do not know where he is? Other things are more important than staying warm." He was so loud that the other people stopped what they were doing and turned around to hear him yelling at his sister. His face was red, and as he yelled, he kept pointing at her. As he was ready to continue, his mother came over and pulled him by the arm and looked him in the eyes with a look that Levi had never seen from her before. She said, "That will be enough. You will not talk to your sister in this manner. I do not think you realize that we all are having a difficult time, and she is just trying to pass the time. She is young and does not understand what is happening. Your yelling at her is not going to help."

Levi looked in his mother's eyes, and for the first time in his life, she was angry with him — in fact, disappointed. His mother's eyes filled with tears and his emotions welled to the surface. He broke down and cried, almost uncontrollably. As his mother held him in her arms, she kissed his head and whispered, "God has done great things for us, and He will see us through this. I know that you did not mean to yell at your sister." As she held him, she kept whispering, "It is okay. Do not worry. It is all going to be okay, so stop crying Levi." He looked over at his sister who was also in tears. She did not know why Levi was so mad at her, but in all of the times they had been together, not once had he ever yelled at her. By this time, all of the women had surrounded them and were trying to comfort the family. One of the women picked Eidel up, and held her, and comforted her with soft words in her ear, "Do not worry my little one. It is all going to be alright. You will see. Your father will be home soon, and we can all celebrate once he arrives."

Levi was embarrassed by what had happened. He was a very proud young man and losing his temper and yelling was not normal for him. He had been angry before, but not like this. All his frustrations surfaced against his sister. Levi regained his composure, and everyone calmed down. They returned to preparing the evening meal. The men were trying to decide what to do. The afternoon was growing late with no sign of the lost men. Levi desired to be part of the conversation on what to do and who should go, but the elders felt it was better left up to the men to decide. Levi was concerned that they would not go out to search for his father and the others, but he would not get a vote on this. So he stood at the entrance looking to the west once again as far as he could see.

Over the hillside, he noticed something moving, but it was only the brush moving with the water that had flooded the area, making it appear that people were moving in the bushes. As the clouds completely cleared, the sun lowering in the sky made seeing into the evening almost impossible. The humidity and the dampness which hung in the air made Levi's clothes heavy, causing him to sweat. Because of all the heavy clothes, Levi went back in to change and noticed that his mother was preparing some food—dates, nuts, and fruits—to eat, since little else was available. Their store was almost depleted, but since they were only a day away from Jerusalem, this would be sufficient for them. Because Levi was a growing young man, he had to be hungry. When he walked up to the table, she told him to sit and eat. He refused saying that he would eat when his father returned. Right now he was going back to the corner to pray again for his safe return. His mother knew that he needed his strength; however, she did not argue with him about his prayer time. Batel and Eidel sat on the ground to eat what they could, leaving something for Levi and Dovid. Batel said to her daughter, "Let us make sure we store some for your brother and father when he arrives home. It should not be long now. It is getting late, and your father knows I worry, so he will be here soon."

Levi again spent time prostrate on the ground, praying to God for the safe return of his father and the others. He continued to seek God's answer to his prayer. Levi prayed, "God the Father of Abraham, Isaac, and Jacob, I pray you will hear my prayer." Levi prayed from Psalms, "*Why are you cast down, O my soul? And why are you disquieted within me? Hope in God, for I shall yet praise Him, the help of my countenance and my God.*"

"Lord, I have prayed both day and night, and you still have not answered me. I seek your wisdom and under-standing, and yet, as I ask, I receive none. God, you are the Most High God, full of love for your people. I pray that you hear my prayer and grant me this request." As Levi laid there in silence he waited for God to give him understanding and peace. He remained still, for he was tired and weak from all that had happened, and as he closed off his mind to all the worry and pain, a peace came upon him. His arms felt lighter, and his head was cooled by a light breeze. Suddenly, it was as if the entire world had stopped and was frozen in time. Levi, in the quiet of the moment, heard a voice in his head that said, "Be still and know that I am the Lord. Levi, I have heard your prayers. Go in peace and wait upon the Lord, for He will give you wisdom in His time."

As Levi recognized his surroundings, he noticed a great aroma in the air—a flower smell that simply overwhelmed him. The odor was like nothing he had ever smelled before—a fragrance so sweet, and yet, somehow soothing. The cool air came from behind his head. The voice also seemed to come from behind him. Indeed, this event was very strange; he had *never* experienced anything like this before in his young life.

Levi lifted his head and glanced around, but saw no one close enough to have spoken to him. He noticed that the air was hot again, and he began to sweat once more. What was going on? Had he fallen asleep for a few moments? Was this all a dream? The aroma still hung slightly in the air, but when he went and asked his mother if she smelled it, she answered. "No;" his sister said the same thing. The odor was present; he could smell it, but it was not there. He thought to himself, "Was God talking to me? Could God have answered my prayers, and if so, where is my father?" He thought back on what he heard, "Be still and know that I am God. I have heard your prayers—go in peace. Wait upon the Lord, for He will give you wisdom in His time." What time, what peace? None of this made any sense. He seemed to feel more anxious than before. He then looked at his mother. Should he tell her what had just happened? Would she even believe him? Should he say anything at all to anyone? Besides, who would believe him?

Just a few days before, his mentor and friend Ishaq had been telling people that he had seen the Messiah, and they basically laughed at him. This would be worse. He thought, what would I say? "Hey, guess what? I was praying to God, and He talked to me like He did to Moses and Abraham and told me to wait upon the Lord and He would give me peace in His time?" He imagined people laughing at him and saying, "Sure Levi, God talked to you, and the smell—was it heaven? You were dreaming. Why would God talk to you? If He were going to talk to anyone, He would talk to the High Priests or the learned men, not a thirteen-year-old boy." So Levi decided to keep the incident to himself, but he felt different for some reason. He felt certain that his father was safe, and he just really needed to trust God and His mercy.

By now, Levi realized that his sister was still frightened and cold. As he was getting ready to sit and pray again, he looked at her and realized she was having a difficult time. He needed to pray, but he also had sympathy toward his sister. The fact remained, as the man of the house he needed to spend some time with her. So, with the realization that just an hour or so ago he was yelling at his sister, he turned around and went back and said to Eidel, "How are you doing?" "Are you cold?" She told him, "Yes," and he made her remove her wet outer garment and took off his and wrapped it around her. His cloak had dried from being outside, so it helped her warm up a little. He said to her, "Come outside with me where the sun will help warm you." She did not want to leave her mother, but her mother insisted that she go with Levi. As they walked outside and the warm sun hit her face and she was warmed. Levi told her, "Let us go over by the hillside and see if we can see our father coming."

Levi finally realized that he was not the only one who was worried. His sister might be younger, but she also was very worried about their father. As they reached the hillside some twenty feet from the cave, they sat down. Levi told her to look to the west toward the sun where it was lowering into the horizon. Because that would most likely be the area from which their father would be coming. The more Levi sat with her, the more he realized that his sister did not have many friends with whom to talk. Mostly, he was the one she played with all the time. As her big brother—the most important person in her life besides her parents, she needed to spend time with him now. They spent a lot of time together in the past and on this journey, and she looked up to her brother. So, right now, she needed for him to spend time with her. She really was not so much cold as just lonely. He realized that during all the time he had spent praying and thinking about their father, she had no one with whom to talk or pass the time.

As they sat, the conversation did not go far. They just talked about her spending time with him. The siblings continued to look to the west for their father, and Eidel put her head against his shoulder and quietly sighed. Levi looked at her and said, "You know Eidel, God has answered your prayer and mine already. He has told me so Himself. You have no need to worry about our father. He will be home shortly, and we can have confidence in God's mercy and love. All we need is to be patient and wait upon His wisdom." The funny thing is that, as Levi said this to his sister, he had a peace ascend within him that now, for the first time, he also believed. He looked up to heaven and smiled and thanked God for His kindness and love. He thought to himself that when his father returned, he would praise God both day and night and tell all who would listen that the God of Abraham, Isaac, and Jacob had answered his prayers. All praise and honor be His forever and ever!

The elders decided to go out and search for the men, but Levi was not allowed to go. They felt that this was a job for the older men. The task could be dangerous, and since he was not familiar with the terrain, he and the other young men could get hurt. Levi was not happy, but he understood. Just a short while ago, he was angry that they did not include him in the discussion, but now he was okay with the decision they had made. The men took their lantern poles with them. They requested the cave be kept lit as much as possible so that they could have a reference point as they went out into the blackness of the night. At least Levi could help with that. So as the men left, he and his sister stayed on the higher rock and watched as the men headed to the west. They watched as long as they could before the sun set and dusk had fallen. Batel walked out to be with her children and sat down with them on the rock. They just sat there peacefully watching for the men to give them a sign that they might see the others, but as the three of them sat, Batel was captured by the beauty of the evening's sunset. The backdrop of the wilderness and color of the sun as it set on the mountains changed from brown and green to reddish green. It was so beautiful that it was like a painting made by God Himself. A peace came over her as she sat there. They noticed that the wind had died down and the air was crisp again—no longer muggy. Peace so invaded the area that they knew everything was going to be alright. Levi looked at his mother as she stared ahead, and the reflection of the moon rising in her eyes, as it reflected her beauty, made the setting magical. His mother was beautiful and her face glowed. Levi thought to himself, "I have always seen Mother working and cleaning and cooking, but for the first time I see her beauty."

They lit the torches for the search party and also as a protection from stray animals that might wander their way. Then, it must have been around 9:00 in the evening when the party returned. They were anticipating them coming back with the men, but the only people who returned were the members of the search party. They said they did not see anything at all that would indicate the missing men were close. Several members of the group were disappointed, cried, and began to worry. Levi stood up and spoke to the entire group: "Please fear not, for the Lord is with us. Our family members are okay, and we need to trust that God will return them to us unharmed." They looked at him strangely, asking, "Who are you to speak this way, and how can you be so sure of what you say?" Levi looked at them with certainty and said, "Because He has promised to keep His children safe and to see us through all things. God is going to see our families through this, and the missing will return to us as we have prayed, for I know it." Several people got angry with Levi and spoke amongst themselves saying, "How can this boy be so certain? What makes him so sure that we should believe him?" Many of the people were now shouting at the boy, when his mother jumped in and said, "My son has done nothing wrong but believed in what the Scriptures have told us to believe. You have no right to be angry with him. He is confident in the Lord and knows that all that has been promised will be fulfilled." Levi once again stood his ground and looked at the group and said that the Lord Himself had told him to be still and wait that He had heard his prayer, and that it would be answered in His time. The crowd was shocked and backed away, inquiring, "You have talked to the Lord? He has spoken to you? How can this be? You should pray for forgiveness for these lies." They all were so busy yelling at each other, some believing what Levi had said, and others saying that this could not be true, that as the yelling got louder, a voice from outside of the cave thundered, "What is all the shouting about?" Immediately everyone looked to the opening of the cave and was astonished by what they saw. The missing men had returned with the animals and meat to eat. The surprised group all turned toward the men, expressing joy at their return. None were more joyful than Levi and his mother. They ran to Dovid and held him so tight that he had to ask them to stop for a minute. They did not want to let go. Batel was so overcome with joy and relief that she cried and cried. The more Dovid told her to stop crying, the more she cried. Levi got on the ground face down in the midst of the people and cried out to God with great loud praises, thanking Him for bringing the men home. He shouted how awesome his God was for answering their prayers. He went on and on singing praises to the Lord for returning his father safe and sound.

After the reunion, all the families sat down to eat. Needless to say, Dovid and the others were famished. When they finished supper, Dovid and Levi sat in the corner and talked quietly about what had happened. Levi was still excited and kept touching his father's face with his hand. Looking at him as he had never done before, and all the while caressing his face, he said, "How great our God, the Father of Abraham, Isaac, and Jacob is for allowing me to have my father back." Levi went on to tell his father about the search and what happened while he was gone. He told his father everything, including the situation with his sister, how angry he got and how he treated her badly. He explained how he tried to be the man of the house, as Dovid had instructed, but Levi confessed to his father that he had not done such a good job. All he could think about was that his father was missing. With tears in his eyes, Levi went on to tell his father that he must be disappointed in him for not being stronger, and doing a better job at helping around the camp. Dovid looked at his son, as emotion swelled within him. He realized that his son must have been terrified. Not knowing where they were or what had happened to them must have been horrifying! Dovid, looking into his son's eyes, said, "Levi, you are my son, and no matter what, I will always love you. Please do not worry. I am more proud of you than you could ever know. You are a very strong young man and have a great heart for God and our family. What father could be more proud than I? From the day you were born, you have always been a strong-spirited child. Your mother and I named you Levi because when you were born, you cried and screamed so loud that it was like listening to a lion roar. Thus, the name fit. Levi, you have a special gift, and God will see you through, but know this—no matter what, no matter when, I will always be here for you, and I will always be proud of you. God loves us in the same way, so you have no reason to either be upset or feel guilty. You are a great son, brother, and friend to all, and I am so proud of you." With that, he kissed Levi on the forehead and then hugged him lovingly.

Levi looked up at Dovid again and began to tell him how he prayed and how he waited patiently on the Lord as he was instructed to do. He told his father about hearing God's voice telling him that He had heard his prayer and to wait upon the Lord. He told his father that he had told the others about hearing the voice, and they got mad at him. He said they basically called him a liar and were getting angry, because they could not believe that God would have spoken to a young boy. Dovid asked Levi for more details and Levi explained how he prayed, when he prayed, and what he prayed about. A strange look came across Dovid's face, actually more a look of terror, and then coldness came over him the more Levi spoke. Dovid asked his son, "When did this encounter happen with the voice?" Levi told him how he thought it was like a dream. In fact, Levi, for a while, did not realize it was a voice because he felt like he was asleep on the floor of the cave.

The more Dovid questioned him, the more his expression changed. Levi looked at his father and asked, "Father, why are you so serious looking? Have I said something wrong?" "No, no," said his father, "I was just wondering because it just seems...." At this point, Levi cut him off saying, "But I did not make it up Father. I really did not." In an attempt to reassure his son that nothing was wrong, Dovid said, "I know that Levi. I am not saying that I do not believe you." Dovid thought to himself, "Not only do I believe you, I know it is true." He thought to himself, "I heard the same voice as I was struggling in the water—a voice that told me to grab on to the branch of the tree as I was being washed away by the flood. I heard the voice clearly, and yet the voice seemed like a dream. When I took hold of the branch and was able to get to shore, just before I would have been swept away into the Jordan River, I looked around, and saw no one at all. So who could have told me to grab the branch?" But, he did not want to talk about it, so he told Levi, "I believe you. Do not worry. I am just tired now from the long journey and I need some rest." So Levi and Dovid changed the subject, but Dovid could not get the events of the last few hours off his mind. They talked for awhile longer, and then Dovid announced to his family that he was tired and needed to get some rest because tomorrow they had to leave early for Jerusalem.

Dovid kissed Eidel goodnight; however, she held him for so long that when he tried to put her down, she would not let go. He told her, "Eidel, please get down. I am alright, and I am not going anywhere. It is okay. My child, please get down and I will help you get ready for bed." Eidel looked into her father's eyes and said, "You do not know that Father. Levi told me it is not up to us, but to God, and I do not know God that well, so I am not going to let you go. Wherever you go, I will go also." Dovid chuckled out loud and told his beautiful little girl that it was okay, not to worry, that God would not take him away from her. But, Eidel hung on for dear life and squeezed him even harder. Batel lifted Eidel off her father's neck and told her to clean up and get ready for bed. Dovid thought to himself how blessed he was to have his children and wife. This very thought brought tears to his eyes once again. He, too, was tired and wanted to get some sleep. Batel came over, and as they were readying for bed, she said, "You did not tell me what happened out there. Why did it take so long to get back?" Dovid glanced at Batel and at first said nothing. Locating the animals and getting them back took a long time. But, he did not dare mention the events that took place for fear she would think him crazy. One thing was for certain. He heard a voice while he was being carried away, and whoever or whatever it was, had saved his life. Now he was tired and needed some sleep. He kissed his beautiful wife good night and they retired.

In the middle of the night—toward early morning, Dovid heard the voice again! Only this time the voice said, "Tell your son and family what I have done for you." The voice was so clear and loud that it woke Dovid from his sleep and had him so shook up that he jumped up off the ground and yelled. The commotion woke up many of the people, who looked around and went back to sleep. However, for Dovid that was another story—how could he sleep now?

Dovid tossed and turned. He was sweating, and the more he tried to sleep, the more anxious he became. Batel turned to her husband and said, "What is it dear? What is troubling you?" "Nothing," he said. "Go back to sleep, I just had a bad dream." So she turned over and went back to sleep. Dovid, on the other hand, tried and tried, but could not get that voice off his mind. "Was it God? It must have been, who else could it be? This is nonsense," he said to himself. "Why would God be talking to me? I am nobody. I am nothing but a humble pottery maker. I am just tired from the trip and need some sleep. I will feel better in the morning." So, off to sleep he went. As he slept, he had a dream in which he saw his old friend Ishaq who said to him, "Dovid, why do you not obey the Lord? Trust in the Lord your God and be of good courage and know that your prayers will and have been answered."

Dovid, in his dream asked, "How is it that you who are dead would come to me with this message?" Ishaq told him, "The Lord your God has sent me to tell you to listen to His commands. He has already shown you His power and glory when you were lost and alone, when He pulled you out of the raging waters. Dovid, you know the Scriptures, '*Hear O Israel, the Lord our God, the Lord is one. Love the Lord your God with all your heart, and with all your soul, with all your mind, and with all your strength.*' You will soon see His glory and power again in the city of Jerusalem." Puzzled, Dovid asked Ishaq, "What does this mean? Why are you telling me this? Why are you here? You are scaring me. How do you know about the flooding? Was it you who helped me?" As Ishaq began to fade away, Dovid asked, "Where are you going?" With that, Ishaq replied, "Dovid, listen to your heart and obey the Lord." Dovid said, "Do not go. Wait, I need to know what you are talking about. Wait, please do not go."

Dovid was awakened from his wife shaking him. "Dovid, wake up. You are dreaming," said Batel. "Were you having that bad dream again?" Dovid looked at his wife and said, "I was visited by Ishaq." She looked at him and began to feel frightened. "Tell me what he said." Dovid took Batel's hands in his, looked her in the eyes, and began to relate what happened. He explained in detail about the dream and what Ishaq said. He also explained what happened earlier in the night, how God had spoken to him, and, as he continued, he began to shake. She held his hands tightly, but it did no good. She could not stop his shaking. He went on to tell her about the voice of God and how he was told his prayers had been answered. He told her about what actually happened in the wilderness while looking for the animals—how he was swept out by the flood and was drowning, when a voice told him to grab onto the branch. Batel fell on her knees confessing, "God has come to our home. How blessed are we to be called the children of God?" Batel also told her husband that she too had heard a voice and that it said the same thing—that their prayers had been answered. She did not know what it meant, but she was certain that it had to do with her husband coming back to her and that she also had been told that in Jerusalem, she would see God's glory and power. After relating to Dovid what she had been told, he also fell on his knees, thanked God, and asked for His blessing on their family as they went forth to the Holy City.

Dovid was overwhelmed with what had occurred, and a fear came over him that he had never felt before. At that exact moment, he realized that God had been in their midst, but more importantly, God had saved his life, and he realized that God must have some reason for doing so.

Dovid began to pray out loud, "Lord I am a sinful man. Please accept your humble servant's plea. Please wipe away my sins and restore me to your grace." As he continued to ask God for blessings on his family and the entire group, he began to cry, and as he continued to pray, it became louder and more intense. At this point, Dovid could no longer remain kneeling and fell face down on the ground sobbing. Batel, alongside him, attempted to lift him, but could not. He was a big man, and she could not budge him. During this time, the children awakened and heard the commotion and realized that their father was crying. They jumped up and ran to him. Levi and Eidel both could not understand why he was crying. Levi began to pray, "Lord in your loving kindness, please help my father and heal him. Please bend down and hear my prayer for him." As Levi prayed, Eidel was crying and trying to pull her father's head up. Dovid heard Levi's prayers and picked up his head. As he did so, he could barely see out of his eyes which were filled with tears. He tried to squint and clear them, but he still could not see. Dovid, now on his knees, stretched out his arms. Levi came running to his father, and Eidel was hanging on her father's neck, clinging to him from behind. Dovid now held his son so tightly and continued to repeat in his ear softly at first, "I am sorry. I did not tell you yesterday that I knew about your vision and that I also had a similar vision. I am so sorry I did not tell you when you asked." Levi asked him what he was talking about. He could not understand him that well. Levi asked him to explain what he meant by having experienced a similar vision and what God had to do with it.

By now, many of the group was awake and listening to the family talk. How could they sleep with all that noise? They did not intrude, but those who were close could hear clearly what Dovid was telling his family. Dovid continued, "Yesterday when we were talking about what happened in the wilderness, you told me of your story about how you felt God had spoken to you, telling you that your prayers had been answered, correct?" Levi said, "Yes, that is true but, what does this have to do with you?" "I was out in the field looking for the animals and walking close to the running waters when I slipped and fell in. I could not get my balance and the more I tried to get up, the more tired I became. The water was running so fast, it was all I could do just to stay afloat. As I neared the Jordan River, I was really beginning to panic, and I heard this voice which said, 'Grab on to the branch.' I turned, and right behind me was a branch floating in the water. I did as the voice had commanded, and I was able to get close enough to the branch that was caught on some debris and it stopped me! I did not see the branch before, nor did I see anyone on the shoreline, but the voice was loud and clear." As the conversation continued, they tried to pin down what time this had happened, and both Dovid and Levi realized that it happened to both of them around the same time of the day. This was truly a miracle, and that was when Levi said, "I was also told that my prayers had been answered." Dovid heard his son, quickly looked at his wife, and then realized that they had been blessed. Eidel asked her father, "Are you getting sick? Do Levi and I need to pray for you again? Dovid looked at his beautiful daughter and smiled and said, "No dear, your father is just fine. We are all fine."

As they sat in silence, the sun was rising. The haziness of the gray had turned to turquoise on the horizon, and as the sun climbed into the sky, they could pick out the different shades of the color red as the sun hit the clouds. This glorious sunrise was one of the most wonderful they had ever experienced. They just sat looking at the sun, and in a peaceful quiet moment, Dovid said to his family, *"The Lord is my rock and my refuge, whom shall I fear?"* Batel exclaimed that God had painted the heavens with His hand to show them the beauty of His work and creation. They all agreed that no one could remember seeing the sky so beautiful or brilliant as this morning. Dovid looked at his family and said, "What do you think God has in store for us in Jerusalem? What do you think God meant when he told us that we would see His glory revealed in the Holy City?" They had no idea, but one thing they did know was that God would be with them, and they had been blessed by His presence on their journey.

DAY FOUR

✝

Now behind schedule, it being the day of the Sabbath, and still very tired from the prior day's events, the entourage resumes their journey. The men were concerned because if they were not going to reach the Holy City before sundown, they would have to survive in the wilderness one more entire day and evening Their clothes were still heavy with dampness from the rain and with the amount of travel that lay ahead of them, this day would be particularly difficult. The hardest part of the trip was still ahead of them. They had to make it over one additional steep hillside and then travel down to the Kidron Valley in order to make it to the tent areas just outside the Temple. By now, more and more people would be arriving and making the trip even slower. With everything that had already occurred on the trip, this last leg was going to be a real challenge. Many of the people had been this way before; however, they had never experienced the trail after heavy rains. Most of the people did not realize how muddy it was going to be and they could not anticipate the mudslides they would encounter. This was not even part of their thought process. Nonetheless, they headed out toward Jerusalem as early as possible. They wanted to get there before all the good land locations had been taken, and they wanted to be as close to the Temple as possible. This was important because the closer they got, the more time they could spend in the city bartering, praying, and seeing old friends.

As they headed up the hillside which was, in itself, a very difficult terrain rising eleven-hundred and fifty feet high, they had to make adjustments heading left, then right, to avoid muddy areas. The animals and the carts experienced slow-going and, in a few places, they got stuck. Stopping just put them further behind schedule. The men had to use their energy to get them out of the mud. Many people were slipping in the wet areas, and snakes and other insects were displaced because of all the water. This made it extremely dangerous as well. Dovid instructed his family, particularly his daughter, to watch for movement on the ground in front of her or to the sides. If she spotted anything that looked like it was moving, she was to stop and let her father know. As they headed up the mountain, their feet were filled with mud, and the soles of their sandals were so muddy they could hardly hold traction. Dovid looked down and noticed that, as he stepped, the mud covered his feet and went up to his ankles. Everyone was experiencing problems. The closer they moved to the top, the more difficulty they encountered.

It was now late afternoon and they were still about two hours away from Jerusalem where they would begin preparations for the Sabbath. The greatest part of the trip was about to occur just as they reached the top of the mountain. They would look down and see the Holy City, a sight that is like nothing else. To view this paradise from above and to see the Holy City in all its glory was like nothing else in the world. To look down and see the Holy Temple and the deep valley was absolutely breathtaking. The people could be seen moving about among all the tents. From this vantage point, the Temple appeared small, but it was anything but small.

At the top Dovid was overwhelmed by the view, and so were his family as well as the others on the journey. They stopped for a moment to take in its beauty and were in awe of its size. As they stood there, Dovid was reminded that just a few short hours ago, he almost did not make this trip. That if it had not been for God, he would be dead. Now he was standing there taking in everything from a different viewpoint. He reflected on what God had told him. The anticipation of something great happening in the city began to excite him. This Passover was going to be something special, not only because of what had happened to his family, but because he felt closer to God than he had ever felt in his life. But for now, he and his family were taking in the view and were spellbound by its magnitude and beauty. He began to tell his family what made this city so amazing. "Did you know that during Passover, the Holy City will hold a great many people?" Dovid estimated that there would be over 250,000 people in the city at the same time. The Temple and the Court held many important features, including the Court of the Gentiles, the Inner Temple of Solomon, and Antonia Fortress, to name a few." He continued, "Did you also know that the Temple itself is a massive 150 feet high and 150 feet wide, facing the east and is made of white marble and its decorations are pure gold?"

On the outside was the Court of Gentiles, a huge rectangular area, enclosed on the east, north, and west by stately colonnades with sixty-foot high columns, and on the south by a three-story-high basilica called the Royal Porch. Worshippers entered the Court of Gentiles through any one of nine gates which stand at intervals around the Temple enclosure, welcoming Gentiles as well as Jews. Levi now possessed a great interest in the Temple and asked his father, "What is that on the north side of the Temple?"

Dovid explained that Antonia's Fortress, which is connected to the Court of Gentiles, stands on the north side of the Temple. The Roman soldiers stationed there were always on the alert for trouble in the Temple compound. Levi asked what the four high towers were used for, and Dovid told him they were used to hold the robes for the High Priests. They were released only on important religious feast days. Dovid possessed a great understanding of the city and the Temple. He had been coming to the Holy City since he was a young boy himself. His knowledge had been handed down for generations from his father and his father's father. Dovid was excited to be able to pass on his understanding of the great city to his own family.

The group, after standing there awhile admiring the view, headed down the mountain toward the city and through the valley toward the tent area. They were hoping to get a good location to ensure access to the gates into the city as well as the Temple itself. Dovid instructed Levi, "When we get to the tent area, I want your help in picking out our spot. It is important for you to learn where the best spots are and how to locate them." Levi was excited to be part of this, but his mind was still thinking about what happened yesterday and what God had in store for them. Levi thought to himself, "What did God mean that His glory would be revealed in the Holy City?" Dovid asked his son, "What is the matter? You do not look happy about helping me pick out the location for our stay." "No, Father," Levi exclaimed, "I am very happy to help. In fact, I consider it a great honor." "Then, what is wrong?" "I am just thinking about what God will reveal while we are in the city." Dovid took a deep breath and pulled on his beard as he said, "I am thinking the same thing Levi, the same thing. We must be patient and wait on the Lord." Levi shouted and said, "That is what He said, 'wait upon the Lord and His glory will be revealed.'" David continued, "Let us get to the valley and get set up before sundown so that we can begin the Sabbath and honor God for his love and kindness to see us through this trip."

The valley had become a very wet, muddy area. After all the rain and wind, many of the tents were blown down and were covered with water. Dovid realized that, had they arrived a day earlier, they would have been in the same situation. The biggest task now was to find a piece of dry land that was high enough so that if it rained again and the area flooded, they could stay somewhat dry. Dovid and Levi searched for a location that was just right. Dovid led Levi to a location he had used in the past and that he knew would withstand the weather in the event it turned bad again. "Levi, let us head to the far southeastern side of the Temple along the Kidron Valley so that we can have access from the Huldah Gates which is the best area to enter the Temple. The gates have four large entrances, allowing easy access, and we will be on the other side from Antonia's fortress where the Roman army is stationed. The farther from them the better, but more importantly, it will make it easy for us to do our bartering in the main part of the city."

Dovid pointed to a spot and said, "There, over there Levi. What do you think?" Dovid had been in this area and used it several times before. Levi was sure this was a good spot. "We need to set up camp quickly. The day is almost behind us, so let us see how quickly we can do this." Levi said to his father, "We do not have much time because it is almost dusk." Batel and Eidel also helped to move things along. Luckily, they got it all done just in time. The families had prepared enough food for the next day, because the Sabbath had begun at the sounding of the horn and would end at sundown tomorrow. Once supper was done, Levi went off in the corner and prayed with a lamplight. He searched the Scriptures for anything he could remember about God's promises and foretelling of when the Messiah would come and what they could expect.

Since arriving in Jerusalem, they had begun to hear more and more about this man named Jesus. They also had heard that he had been seen raising a man from the dead, a man named Lazarus. Surely, the Messiah would be able to do this and more. But people were saying that this man, Jesus, was a fake, a demon-possessed man. Why would God send the Messiah in this man, and if He were the Messiah, everyone should recognize Him, and He would free His people once and for all. It was not clear to Levi what was right and what was wrong. One thing is for sure—God had told him that His glory would be seen in the city, and he was looking forward to seeing what that was. As Levi finished his prayers, his father came up behind him and told him it was time to get some sleep because they had plenty to do in the morning. Levi asked him what they had to do, since no one would be bartering during the day. Dovid said, "We are going to the Temple to pray early, and then you and I will meet with a group of wise men who tell the stories of Jesus, and I want to know who he is and what he has done." Levi told his father, "I had the same thought. I would like to see this man and hear more about him also. Father, do you think this is the Messiah? Do you think this is what God was talking about when we were told about His glory?" "Levi, I do not know, but I do know that everyone is talking about this man and what He has done. I want to know more and learn more. If He is the Messiah, we will know it."

The Passover was less than a week away now, and they needed to prepare and obtain the necessities for the feast. Dovid was really proud of the lamb they had brought for their sacrifice this year. This animal was the best they had ever brought. So much had to be done with little time and space. One of the women in the group told Batel that one of the reasons for such a larger-than-normal crowd was because the people had heard that the man named Jesus was present. They had been told that He had raised the dead and healed the crippled and the blind. They were hoping that they would see Him and learn more about Him. Batel also told them that, even in the town of Scythopolis, they had heard of Him. Some were even saying that He was in town not too long ago.

People from all over the area, even from other parts of the world, were here for this Passover to hear Him and see Him. They were hoping to see the miracles and judge for themselves who this man was. The vast number of people this year was going to make bartering, and obtaining what was needed, more difficult than usual. Batel told the woman she hoped that the merchants would not run out of items because of the larger than usual crowd.

One by one all the oil lanterns were being extinguished and the tent area grew dark. Yet, a little light still shone in on their tent as the people next to them had not put out their lamps completely. So Levi watched as the area outside his tent grew darker, except for the one light. Levi thought to himself that God was the light. He began to think of what God must see from heaven; all these lights down here where people were preparing to celebrate the Passover holiday. Levi surmised that when God looked down from heaven, the lights must appear to Him like the stars He had flung into the heavens. He reflected on the Scriptures which say, *"Your word is a lamp to my feet and a light to my path,"* and also, *"The Lord is my light and my salvation whom shall I fear?"* As he continued to think through the Scriptures, he realized that the light was not any dimmer in the tent next to them; rather, it seemed to grow brighter. His eyes were so fixated on the light that, at one point, it was so bright that he had to close his eyes. When he opened them again, it was out. He thought it strange, but nonetheless, it was out. Finally, he prayed this prayer: "Lord, I ask your blessing on my family and all those who have come to celebrate this Passover, and that we have no fear, for you are the God of our fathers— Abraham, Isaac, and Jacob." As Levi recited this prayer, he fell asleep. Dovid and Batel slept looking forward to the days ahead and to the Passover. Because they were so tired, they all slept soundly. The only problem they were to incur was with the great number of people, it would make it difficult to move around.

DAY FIVE

✝

The morning dawned, and people were already up and about when Levi awoke. Still the air was cold from the prior evening, and as he yawned and took in a deep breath, the cold air gave him chills. His eyes barely open, he thought to himself, "There is no privacy here. Everyone is so close and you can hear what everyone else is talking about." He listened as he was lying on the ground. He could hear many things—everything from people praying to talking about their children, from the physical problems they were dealing with to conversations about Jesus of Nazareth, the self-proclaimed Messiah. He knew it was time to get going, so he raised himself up and noticed that his family was already outside the tent getting preparations underway for the coming day.

The family ate their breakfast meal prepared that prior evening. The meal was ready as was customary. The elder members of the group were up first, then the younger ones. The good night's sleep and seeing the food made Levi so hungry that he not only ate his own food, but his father gave him a portion of his as well. Dovid looked at Levi and Eidel and smiled and said, "God has blessed us beyond our expectations, and we are grateful, for with each generation comes great promise and expectations." Dovid looked seriously at both of his children, and rubbing his face with his left hand said, "I am proud of both of you. Each of you has been blessed by our God. Praise to our God, the Father of Abraham, Isaac, and Jacob." With that, they finished their meal and got ready to head out for prayers.

The remaining part of the day was filled with time spent with family and neighbors discussing the Passover and God's blessings on them. The day was very unusual for the family. They got to spend time with other members of the town, including friends and loved ones, talking about the Scriptures and many other things. Levi was especially happy because he got to work on his memorization of the remaining books of the Torah. He practiced and practiced and asked his father to go over some specific areas with which he was having a hard time. The evening came and went, as was normal, until they heard the sound of the horn, again signifying that the Sabbath was over. Then, once again, they turned their attention back to things of the day and what they would be doing the rest of the week.

DAY SIX

✝

As they were preparing to head to town, Azel, a friend of Dovid's came by to tell Dovid that he and his family were taking the two-and-a-half mile trip to Bethany where the man, Jesus, was staying with a friend named Lazarus. He asked if they wanted to come along. Dovid told him no, that they needed to get some materials and supplies, and that even though they would love to see Him, the encounter would have to wait. Levi looked at his father and said, "Please Father. We may never get another chance to see this man. I thought you were hoping to get to see Him. Please, may we go?" Dovid explained that they must go into town and get the supplies. Levi said, "Very well." Azel said, "Dovid, would it be okay if I took Levi with us? He seems so interested in this man, and I would hate to see him miss Him." Levi said, "Thank you for your invitation; however, I must go with my father and do what is necessary for my family." Dovid looked at Levi and said, "Yes, we do have a lot to do, but thank you anyway."

Azel walked away, and as he did, Dovid turned and called to him, "What time will you be back?" Azel told his friend that they would be back in time for the mid-day meal. After saying, "Very well, have a good trip and be safe," Dovid then turned to Levi and said, "Do not be late getting back." Levi looked at him with a great smile and said, "Thank you Father, but I must stay with you and do what is more important for the family." Dovid said, "Levi, you are going to be a Pharisee, are you not? Yes, then you need to examine all things to better understand what is true. Go my son and be careful and respect what you are told by Azel." "Thank you Father, are you sure? I do not mind staying behind." Dovid looked into his son's eyes wide-open with excitement and said, "Yes, I am sure. Now go before I change my mind. God be with you son, and tell us all about this man when you return." Dovid called to Azel again, "Please take my son with you if you do not mind." Azel smiled and nodded his assent to Dovid.

Levi ran to his mother and told her that he was going with Azel and his family to see Jesus, and he would be back later. He was so excited that he ran off without even saying goodbye. Batel called out to him, "Levi," and he turned and his mother said, "Did you forget anything?" He thought for a moment and said, "Yes! I forgot to bring something for the trip." She said, "No, you forgot to say goodbye to me." He ran back, retrieved something to eat later on the trip, and then kissed her and ran to Azel's tent.

As they began their trip, Azel asked Levi about his studies and how they were progressing. Levi told him that he did not know if he would be able to complete the next step of training right now since his mentor had died. Azel inquired if anyone else might be able to step in and help. Levi replied that he did not think his parents could afford to have him go away right now and study under someone else. Finding someone to tutor you was difficult. Furthermore, he had studied under Ishaq for so long that he did not know anyone else who would be willing to continue his training since he would not have started with them. Azel, making an attempt at small talk with Levi, asked him, "Have you

thought what you will do if you do not become a Pharisee?"
Levi thought for a moment and said, "I will follow in my
father's footsteps and become a pottery maker."

"You know Levi, many of the people around here are
saying that this Jesus is the Messiah and that He speaks of
God as if He is God. Do you believe that this man could be
God? I have heard over the last two days people saying that
He will not come to Jerusalem during the Passover because
many of the Sadducees and Pharisees want to arrest Him."
Levi replied, "People say that he speaks of compassion and
peace. I cannot understand why anyone would want to arrest
him." Azel's wife, Mariska, who was holding her child, asked
Levi, "Do you think that this man, Jesus, is the Son of God?
Since you are very well-versed in the Torah, we thought you
might know." Levi looked down as they walked and said, "I
can only say that the Scriptures say that when the Messiah
comes, we will know it."

Levi continued, "If you follow what has been written by
Isaiah and King David, then we will know when He comes,
for it is written by the Prophet Isaiah, '*I will rejoice in
Jerusalem, and joy in My people; The voice of weeping shall
no longer be heard in her, Nor the voice of crying.*' King
David told us in the Psalms, '*I will declare the decree: The
Lord has said to Me, You are My Son, Today I have begotten
you. Ask of Me, and I will give You The nations for your
inheritance, And the ends of the earth for your possession.*'
So when He comes, He will lead his people once again out
of captivity and will be the King of the whole world. If this
Jesus is truly the Messiah, then He will be a king and lead us
out of captivity and release us from Roman control."

As they made their way up the hill—just past the Mount
of Olives, in the small town of Bethany, a crowd of people
was standing by the entrance to a home. The crowd looked
to be large, and they were all just waiting outside, some
standing others sitting on the ground. As they drew closer,

Azel instructed his family and Levi, "Please stay close. We do not want to be separated. I have been told that the crowds can get angry, and we do not want anything to happen." They all agreed that they would not leave each other's side. When they got to the home, it was obvious that the people living there were of wealth. When seated, Levi noticed that many of the people were sick, crippled, and/or lepers. Azel warned them again to stay close as he did not know what to expect. As they sat, Azel inquired of a woman who was sitting next to them praying as to why people were waiting. She looked at him like he was from another planet. She answered, "We are waiting for the Messiah to come out and hope that He will speak to us and heal the multitudes just as He has been doing all over the area. Do you not know that the Lord, our God is here in this house?" Azel did not seem fazed by this, but pressed further, "How do you know it is Him?" "Because He has given back sight to the blind and healed the crippled, and the man who lives in this house was dead for four days, and our Lord raised him up just recently."

Azel looked at her and inquired, "How do you know He did this? What proof do you have that this happened?" She looked at him and then to the family and said, "Because I was sick for twelve years with uncontrollable bleeding myself that no doctor could stop. He had just come across the sea from Gadarenes, and as He got off the boat, many of us were waiting for Him. The crowd was so large, and while I could not get Him to stop and talk to me, I knew that if I just even touched the Master's garments, I would be healed. Once I did, I felt a healing come to my body. The Lord stopped immediately and asked, '*Who touched my clothes?*' I was so afraid and trembling that I fell at His feet and replied, '*it was I Lord.*' He picked me up and looked in my eyes and said, '*Daughter your faith has made you well. Go in peace, and be healed of your afflictions.*' Since then I have been healed, and I have followed Him everywhere I can." Azel then asked the woman, "You mean even though you were unclean from the blood you walked though the crowd to get to this man just to make Him unclean? Do you know the penalty for such an act?" "Yes," she exclaimed, "I do. It is stoning, but I did not care. I knew from what I had felt and heard that if I could just even touch His shawl, I would be healed. I did not care if I was stoned for I was desperate. I have had this affliction for 12 years and no one could help me! Have you ever been so desperate that you would risk even death to be free! I had to end this pain once and for all. It was a miracle! The Lord healed me that very moment!" Azel puzzled with her remarks was thinking, "What kind of person heals someone without laying hands on them? What kind of power is this?" Azel then turns to look at Mariska and shrugs his shoulders in a gesture of uncertainty. The woman then continued, "I also saw that man over there whose name is Lazarus." Levi looked and noticed he was standing at the entrance of the home. "He was dead for four days and the Lord raised him too." Levi looked at her and got chills up and down his body because he had seen that look before. Yes, that look was familiar to him; he recognized it from his past. As she stared at Levi, she knew he was taken aback by what she had just said. She then focused on Levi and told him, "Do not be frightened child, there is nothing to fear. The Lord our God has come to save us from the Romans and set us free." At this point, Levi recalled his mentor, Ishaq, who told him all about this man named Jesus who did the things this woman had said. He recognized the same look in Ishaq's eyes, that same demeanor, that same confidence that he had about who this man was.

Mariska, seeing the fear and concern in Levi's eyes, placed her arm around him and told him that it was going to be okay. Levi, as if in a daze, looked at her with an expressionless face and announced in a monotone voice that, "God's power and mercy will be revealed in the Holy City this day." Mariska looked at Levi and then at her husband as if to say, "Who is this boy and where did he hear this?" But, the woman did not even blink when this was said. She looked at Levi and said, "Young man, what you say is correct. You will see for yourself when He comes out. Many here have been here all morning waiting for Him. I brought my friend also who is in need of healing. She just arrived here from Philippi."

Everyone was waiting patiently for Jesus to come out. Excited and impatient to see this man, Levi kept a close eye on the front entrance of the home. The crowd was getting bigger, and then they heard a rumbling from behind. Three men came down the middle of the crowd splitting it and telling the people to move aside. They had to get to the home. They had a donkey with them that no one was riding. Levi thought it strange that they had the animal, which they were not using. When they got close, Levi noticed that the men were very serious and were not of wealth. In fact, they looked rather poor and weak in stature and were not from the local government, yet the people obeyed their requests. The people were asking them to heal them, trying to touch them, and asking them for a blessing. They were trying to get inside the home. After they tied up the donkey, they went inside. Levi asked out loud, "Who are these men that people follow their instructions?" The woman said, "They are with our Lord. There are twelve of them who follow Him and stay with Him everywhere He goes. They are called His disciples."

A few minutes later, the men came out. Now Levi was excited, but all the people stood up, and he had a difficult time seeing anything. He could not see over most of the people. The crowd then got louder, and they all seemed to be moving in the same direction. They headed back the way they came toward Jerusalem. Levi could not see anything except the people in front of him, and they were all pushing and trying to get close to Jesus. He jumped up and down trying to see over the people, but the only thing he could see was the heads of the people walking past. Now frustrated, Levi had forgotten that he was to stay close to Azel and his family. He was not even thinking about that now. His goal was to get a chance to see this man — the man they call the Son of God. Levi tried to push his way to the front of the group, but he was experiencing difficulty. He decided to go low to the ground and see if a way existed to go under the crowd. Finally, he saw an opportunity and tried to slip through. It was difficult, but somehow he got through. A man tried to grab his garments, but missed, and he found himself in the front of the crowd.

Just as he tried to stand up, the crowd moved quickly, tripped him, and he fell. He could not see anything because he was face-down on the ground. Many of the people laughed at him, so he tried to pick himself up and dust off the dirt. A man asked him, "Are you alright?" As he arose, he saw only the man's sandals and white garments. He indicated that he was okay and muttered, "Thank you." He looked up to see this man with a smile on his face who told him, "Be careful and go in peace." Levi did not recognize this man, but his voice appeared calming. He then followed the group right behind them but could not seem to find Jesus. He asked another man walking with him, "Where is the man named Jesus?" The gentleman said, "He was right in front of you. You just talked to Him. He is the one who helped you up." Levi was shocked — how can this be? He did not have a crown or a garment of gold; He did not even look like a king. In fact, Levi thought He appeared to be very unassuming. He thought Him to be a rather short man and not exactly good-looking. The thing that struck Levi most was His hands — how hard they appeared; calloused, brittle and dirty. The only appealing thing about Him was His eyes. They were dark, yet soft and kind. Levi reflected on how bright they were as he felt himself staring into Jesus' eyes and feeling comfortable. How could a king be dressed and look like this? He thought to himself, this man could not be the Messiah. Levi was getting lost in the crowd, so he slowed down and stepped back out of the crowd and began looking for Azel and his family, because, for the first time, he realized that they were not nearby. As he searched through the large group, he saw the old woman walking, and following close behind were Azel and his family. Levi apologized to the family. They said next time for him not to get so far from them, that they had been worried about him. The crowd was making their way toward Bethpage, and as they walked up the hill, the crowd was just ahead of them. He could see Jesus riding the donkey that the disciples had brought Him. He was larger than life on the animal, but in the distance, He was only visible from the back. He was talking to the people, and they were asking Him questions. People were begging along the route for Jesus to stop and heal them. Levi recalled he had never seen anything like this before. The group kept growing larger as the word spread that Jesus was coming to Jerusalem.

As they approached Bethpage, just on the upper side of the hill, on the eastern slope of the Mount of Olives, looking over the city of Jerusalem, the group stopped. Jesus was talking to the crowd. Levi was not able to hear what was being said, but the people were now on their knees looking up at Him. From the distance, they looked like statues frozen or mesmerized by what was being said. It looked as if Jesus was talking to each person individually, but that was impossible because there was somewhere between five hundred to a thousand people standing there. Levi turned to Azel and said, "Can we please hurry? I want to hear what He is saying." Just as they got within earshot, he ran up to get closer, and as he did, Jesus looked directly at Levi. Jesus was weeping and said, "If you, even you, had only known on this day what would bring you peace—but now it is hidden from your eyes. The days will come upon you when your enemies will build an embankment against you, encircle you and hem you in on every side. They will dash you to the ground, you and the children within your walls. They will not leave one stone upon another, because you did not recognize the time of God's coming to you." Levi, at hearing this, was thinking to himself, what does this mean? Then, he realized that the donkey ride had prophetic meaning. He remembered the Scriptures that say, *"For it is written that the Lord will come riding on a colt."* Also the Scripture written by Zechariah's Messianic prophecy stated: *"Rejoice greatly, O Daughter of Zion! Shout, Daughter of Jerusalem! See, your king comes to you, righteous and having salvation, gentle and riding on a donkey, on a colt, the foal of a donkey."* After realizing the significance of Jesus riding on the donkey, he fell to his knees, bowed his head, and prayed to God for his help in understanding what this all means. He was really confused and scared, for just a few minutes ago he did not think the Messiah could be this man. Yet, he fulfilled prophesy and spoke to his heart. "Please help me Lord for your under-standing of who this man truly is."

As he opened his eyes again, Jesus was back on the move heading down the hill toward the Kidron Valley and straight toward Jerusalem. He glanced around and saw Azel and his family, along with the old woman kneeling and praying. When they arose, they said to Levi, "Praise be to God the Father of Abraham, Isaac, and Jacob who has sent the Messiah to free us from bondage again." He looked at the old woman, and now she was gleaming, a smile as wide as her face, yet tears rolled down her cheeks as she got to her feet and said: "Oh, taste and see that the Lord is good; blessed is the man who trusts in Him!" All Levi and the others could say was "Amen."

They followed Him down the hill, but something was different. He was seeing Jesus in a different way now; he tried to look at Him, but he was squinting more. The closer He came, the more glaring it became. He tried to move to the side more, figuring that the sun was hitting Him and that was what was making Him look so bright. But, that had no affect at all. He looked around at the crowd that followed Jesus and noticed that he did not have a hard time viewing them—no, it was just Jesus. Levi looked at Azel and said, "I must be seeing things, but does it look like his garments are bright white?" Azel said, "Yes, I am having a hard time looking at Him, too." Just then Jesus turned around on the colt, and looking around at the crowd, looked directly at Levi and smiled. The closer they got to Jerusalem, the more people were lining the dirt road and cheering Jesus' entry on the donkey. The majority of the people were from the Galilean area. Others were Judean supporters, but they took palms and put their cloaks on the road before Him, shouting, "Hosanna! Blessed is He who comes in the name of the Lord! Blessed be the King of Israel!"

Levi and the others knew that the custom of spreading your outer garments in the path was reserved for royalty. By now, the crowd was shouting to Jesus to save them from the Romans. Jesus looked expectantly at them, waving at them. His disciples were leading the crowd in the chanting of "Blessed is He who comes in the name of the Lord, Hosanna," over and over again. While on the way, some of the Jewish leaders told Jesus to make them stop. Jesus shouted at them, "Even if I did, the stones would cry out." The group was headed toward the eastern side of the Temple. You could see the Towers of the Antonia Fortress ahead. As they crossed over the Kidron Valley and into the Holy City, the crowds grew even bigger. They entered from the eastern gate called Golden Gate. Azel looked as they passed by the Fortress and said in a quiet voice to Mariska, "The soldiers were all at attention and on-guard. They had to believe that this man was going to begin a revolt." Levi overheard what he said to Mariska and realized that he was correct. He had not noticed this at first, but now he could see hundreds of the soldiers all around and standing guard. As they headed in through the gates, it took them directly into the Temple precincts. Again, as Levi followed them in, he remembered that it was foretold that the Messiah would come from the east and enter through the eastern gates.

Once inside, Levi's focus was no longer on Jesus, but on what was in front and around him. He noticed all the merchants and the money changers who were doing business. They were shouting and trying to get the attention of the people to buy their goods. Levi was approached two times by merchants to buy something. The place did not look like a Temple; it looked more like a marketplace. Levi felt strange; he was overwhelmed by many things. First, the loudness—everyone was yelling at the pilgrims. They were bartering and trying to do whatever it took to make their sales. In attempting to figure out what was happening in the Temple, he kept turning around and around hearing all that was going on. It was so loud. Then there were the smells, a distinct odor that he normally smelled in the fields—those of urine and dung were overpowering. Levi looked at Azel and said, "I am feeling sick. Can we go now?" Azel said, "Yes, we promised your father we would have you back by mid-day."

Upon his return, he told his family about all that had occurred, and they were amazed. His father said that he noticed all the soldiers around the Temple and overheard many of the men saying that they did not think that Jesus would show His face in the city because they were going to arrest Him. Many of the people found Him interesting and certainly a prophet; however, they did not agree that He is the Son of God. Levi told his parents about the woman they met and what had happened to her, and how she was healed by Jesus. Levi was very excited and was now talking so fast his parents could hardly keep up. He went on to tell them that he saw the man that had been dead and who was resurrected and was with Jesus. His mother asked, "How can this be? How can anyone who is dead come back? This must be some kind of trick." Levi agrees with her; however, many people saw this and swore that he was dead. But, Jesus called him out of the grave. Batel looked at Dovid and said, "If God can come to us, maybe He can come to this man and give Him the powers to heal people." Levi said, "I saw Jesus up close and He did not look like a king, but two of the prophecies that have been foretold of Him, He has fulfilled. I cannot describe what seeing Him was like. He had a presence like no other. When He spoke, He spoke with authority and power. I have never seen anyone talk to a crowd that large before, and everyone not only heard Him, but felt like He was talking just to them personally. I do not know if He is the Messiah, but He is a powerful man of God."

As the evening came, Levi and his father recalled that which was revealed to them during their pilgrimage and how God spoke to them about His glory that would be revealed there. Levi prayed as he went to bed, "Father in Heaven, if this man is our Messiah, I pray that He shows Himself to all." Dovid also preparing for bed told Batel that he was very interested in what was happening in the city. This man, Jesus, was stirring up a lot of controversy. He said, "If this man is the Son of God, I pray He bless everyone and free us from this captivity and bring prosperity back to His people." Batel agreed and stated that time will tell.

DAY SEVEN

✝

As the seventh day began and the family was getting up, Dovid decided that he wanted to go and talk to his friend, Azel. He told Batel he would be back shortly and where he was going. As he got to their tent, Azel was up and making the fire. Dovid asked him his thoughts on what had happened the day before, and did he think that this man, Jesus, was the Messiah. Azel looked at his friend and said, "I do not know for sure, but I will say this—He knows Scripture, and He has healed many people. The crowds that follow Him are large, and they all believe in what He says. They have seen the miracles themselves." So Dovid said, "Then you think He is the Messiah?" "No, I think He could be. I am not ready to say that just yet. I need more proof to be sure." Dovid asked him, "What will it take for you to really know?" Azel replied, "I will have to see one of these miracles myself and then I will know." Dovid was grateful to him for taking his son and stated, "I cannot thank you enough." Azel said, "Levi was not a problem. He was a blessing, and we learned some things from him about Scriptures. I did not realize he possessed such a vast understanding of God's Word. He will make a good Pharisee." Dovid replied, "God willing, he will complete his studies and make us all proud. I must go. We are heading back to the marketplace. We still have to go to the shops and pick up some small things before the Sabbath this week." Azel bid them a blessing and said, "Peace be with you and your family and have a good day." Dovid went back to the tent and told Batel that he was confused by all that was happening. He said, "All everyone is talking about is this man, Jesus; the Passover is not even the reason that many people are here this week. I cannot remember it ever being this crowded before; they are more concerned with what will happen if He comes into the city than prayer and traditions of the holiday."

Dovid continued, "We are losing our traditions, and if we are not careful, we will lose our identity. How can that man command so much attention and why? According to Levi, He does not look like a king and Azel said he is not sure either, so what is the big deal about this man, Jesus?" Now angry, Dovid was shouting, "If He is the Messiah, then why do some people believe and others do not?" Levi overheard his parents talking, and he told them he was not sure that He was the Messiah, but that He had done some amazing things that only the Messiah or God Himself could do. Levi's father questioned him, "So are you saying that you believe that this could be Him? How can this be? What are we to do, drop all our traditions and ways and follow this man to where, and for what? Our people have been following Moses all our lives. He has given us whatever we need, and he gave us God's commandants to follow. We are about to celebrate the Passover, the time when Moses himself led our people out of captivity by the grace of God, and we are not thinking clearly. All we see is something new or different that makes us believe that God is involved. We are dealing with Satan here I tell you! No other explanation for it exists. Even Pharaoh was able to make a snake out of a stick, so what is different about this man? Perhaps Satan is behind this. I am not going to let our traditions be pushed aside, I cannot do much about others, but for me and this family, we are going to follow God's law."

Batel admonished her husband, "Please calm down, you are making a scene." "Good!" Dovid exclaims. "Maybe I can talk some sense into these people. I must be out of my mind to think that the Messiah would come as this man." Levi jumped in and said, "Father, please do not get yourself upset. God will let us know what is the truth." "Levi, with all your knowledge you cannot be sure yourself. How will God let us know?" Levi answered, "The Lord our God has told us that His mercy would be revealed here, right here in Jerusalem. So let us wait on Him to show us what He has intended for us to see." Dovid, still angry, apologized for the outburst saying, "I am not myself this week. Please forgive me, I do not trust what I do not see." "Father, we need to get going to the city or we will not be able to get the early sales."

Dovid and Levi headed to the market district alongside the western wall of the Temple. Many booths were set up to accommodate the pilgrims who were there to purchase their goods. As Levi and his father headed into the market area, Dovid told Levi he really wanted him to never abandon the traditions of their faith. "Levi, promise me you will not get distracted by all this nonsense about new ways of following God. Do not let these radical people get you distracted from the truth. Promise me Levi." Levi looked at his father and said, "Do not worry. I know the law, and I follow the law, and someday I will be interpreting the law for many who follow." "Thank you, my son. I do not know what got into me before, but I am just passionate about our way of life and the traditions they hold." "I know, I am too," replied Levi.

As they reached the marketplace, it was already crowded, and the people were three and four deep in line. As they stood around and waited to get to the front of the line, they overheard conversations from the people talking about Jesus and what He had done. The tempers were flaring because of the heat of the day, plus the time it was taking to wait in line. Add to that the passionate beliefs on both sides, and it was a recipe for disaster. As they waited, the louder the crowd became; pushing and shoving were the norm. Levi and his father saw the Roman soldiers on horseback coming around the block. They came up and started pushing people around with their horses and breaking up the crowd. People were now yelling and cursing at the soldiers, and Dovid took Levi by the hand and moved into the corner out of the way of the horses and people. The crowd was getting worse, shouting, "Jesus, when will you restore our freedom?" Others shouted out, "Lord, Father of our fathers, help us." Still others just shouted at the soldiers to leave them alone. Levi was frightened by all this, and Dovid was really mad. Looking up at his father, Levi had never seen him this angry before.

As the Roman soldiers broke up the crowd and a few people were arrested and taken away, order was restored. Dovid and Levi were back in line by this time, and the people were talking about the Romans and why God did not do something about this. Why has He forsaken us again and allowed us to be held captive. An old man who was blind and sitting under one of the awnings interjected that if they opened their eyes, they would see God's mercy and glory in front of them. Looking straight ahead, he told them that God has revealed Himself in this man named Jesus. The crowd began to laugh at him and ask, "How would you know, you are blind? You cannot see Him." The laughter grew even louder. The man looked into the heavens and lifted his hands up and told them his prayers had been answered, and blessed is the man who hears His word and obeys it. With that, the blind man turned his head and starred right in the direction of Levi and Dovid. As the crowd ignored him, Dovid, as if to protect his son, placed his arm in front of Levi and his eyes flung wide open from this man's comments, which were similar to the words he heard from God. Now they were being spoken by this blind man and were directed at them.

Dovid turned around with his back to the blind man, not because he was next in line, but because he was frightened by what was said. Dovid, while waiting, thought to himself that he had never before felt so unsure of what to do or fearful for his safety. More importantly, he could not recall a time when the people of Israel were so at odds with each other. After all, they were God's chosen people, and they had a lot for which to be proud and thankful. No reason existed to be angry with each other. Plenty of people had always been present outside of Israel with whom to fight or get angry. Dovid struggled with what was happening in the city of David. Just then, they were at the front of the line, and the merchant asked what they would like. As Dovid started to explain to the man what he needed, he heard the crowd growing louder. Again, this time was different. People were running up and shouting, "Jesus is coming! Jesus is coming!" Everyone stopped to get a look, including Dovid. After all, he wanted to see this man and judge for himself whether or not He was the Messiah. As the people lined the street, all the merchants ceased their selling, and the people stopped buying. All the attention was focused on Jesus and His followers as they passed through.

The crowd was stirring and Dovid peered hard to see Him. His heart was beating fast, and needless to say, he was anxious as they passed. Levi pointed and shouted to his father, "There He is!" Just as he yelled out, Jesus turned toward them and looked at Levi and smiled. Dovid placed his arm around Levi as if to say to Jesus, "This is my son." Jesus was asked to stop and heal the masses, but today He went straight into the gates at the Temple as if He was on a mission. Levi followed Him with his eyes as far as he could, but lost Him just a few feet before the gates, because of the large crowds. The area seemed charged with excitement and the air was filled with different fragrances.

The pilgrims could buy anything: souvenirs, silver amulets, animals, and provisions. The more excited the people became about Jesus the more irritated Dovid became with the people. By this time, he was in the street, turning around and attempting to gain people's attention. He asked them, "Where is your belief in the God of Abraham, Isaac, and Jacob? Moses told us *'To you it was shown, that you might know that the Lord Himself is God; there is none other besides Him.'* O' people of Jerusalem hear the word of our Lord and heed His warnings. Do not be fooled by this man. Your Lord, our God, will deliver you from this oppression. Seek the Lord your God with all your heart, soul, mind, and strength, and you will be set free. Have we not learned from our forefathers that Moses warned us, *'You shall not go after other gods, the gods of the peoples who are all around you (for the Lord your God is a jealous God among you), lest the anger of the Lord your God be aroused against you and destroy you from the face of the earth.'*"

As Dovid was telling this to the people in the streets, they turned to him and asked, "Who are you to tell us what we should believe or do? Where do you come from, and what gives you the right to preach to us?" Dovid became really angry, and one of the Priests came out in the street and told the crowd that what this man speaks is correct. "Read the Scriptures from our Father Moses, and you will see this man speaks wisdom. Do not judge this man for what he says, but judge yourselves for what you have not done. You have let the times and your own personal greed get in the way of the law. I tell you, be watchful for the time may come that you will be destroyed for your lack of your obligations and lawlessness. Do not be fooled by this man, Jesus, who speaks the Scriptures, for even Satan knows the Scriptures well. We must not make this self-proclaimed Messiah an idol, for this was the reason our forefathers were sent into the desert for forty years."

Levi, by now, was surprised. No, he was in shock, because he had never heard his father so passionate about anything. For the most part, he had never seen his father speak about the law in public, much less so powerfully. Yet, in his heart, he entertained some questions about this man, Jesus, and what He was doing. He ran to his father and told him, "Let us go before someone starts a fight. Even worse, we do not want the Roman soldiers to return and arrest you." Dovid, still angry, looked at his son and realized that he was correct. They promptly finished their shopping, picked up the packages and headed toward the Temple.

As they left, some were still shouting at him, "Go home. You will burn in Hell when the Messiah and His army overtake the Romans." Dovid looked at the crowd and realized that he would not be able to convince them to remember their covenant with God. Dovid told Levi, "You see son, these people have given up everything—the law, the tradition, and their love of God, to follow a false prophet." Levi desired to tell his father that he was not sure they were wrong, but this was not the time or place—especially in light of what had just happened. Levi nodded and did not say anything.

As they arrived at the Temple, right in front of the southwest corner, as they were heading back to the tents, they heard a commotion inside. People were running up the stairs which led to the Temple courts and to the Temple itself. By now, Dovid and Levi could hear someone yelling inside. Dovid was already mad, so he told Levi, "Let us go in and see what the commotion is about." They went inside to see what was happening, but as they did, they saw Jesus shouting at the merchants in the Temple who were selling goods and services. Levi watched as a merchant sold a blind man a malnourished ram instead of the fatted ram. Dovid and Levi watched as Jesus became so angry that He began to turn over tables, and the money was strewn everywhere. He opened the dove pens and let them fly away. Then He stopped and looked around, and with fire in His eyes, and with such a loud voice said, "Is it not written: *'My house will be called a house of prayer for all nations? But you have turned it into a den of thieves.'*" As Levi heard this, he was taken aback, and Dovid could not even speak. He was mesmerized by what he saw. The others also did not know what to do because they also knew what Jesus said was correct.

Levi searched the area and noticed Roman soldiers on guard all around the top of the Temple as well as many of the High Priests who watched from a distance. He also noticed that the legion of soldiers located in the Antonia Fortress were now coming out and heading toward them. Dovid and his son were just standing there when they overheard a conversation with two of the Sadducees. One said to the other, "We must get rid of this man." The other added, "We must wait until after the feast or I fear a riot." The first man just nodded as they stepped closer. As Dovid and Levi turned to walk away, they heard the children and others in the Temple chanting, "Hosanna to the Son of David." As they left the Temple, they noticed that not too long after, Jesus and His disciples also left and headed back toward Bethpage.

As Levi and his father headed back to the tents with everything they had bought and experienced, they had a lot to discuss; however, not one word was spoken by either of them. The silence of the walk back was only interrupted by the sound of the walk itself—the sound of people walking along the dirt road and returning after a day of bartering. They heard many people speaking exhortations to God for their blessings, while others spoke of Jesus and what He did in the Temple. Most were praising Him for what He had accomplished. Some were saying that when Jesus overturned those tables and all that money spilled everywhere, it was a Passover feast in itself. "Our King is here, He will lead us once and for all, and He must be God. No one did anything to stop Him, neither the merchants nor the Romans."

Dovid was so tired from the day that he did not have the energy to argue with them. He just ignored them as if he was left with his own thoughts about what took place. He kept thinking back to the events of the day. First, he thought about how he spoke in public, the words he used, and his being argumentative with the people. He had never in his life done anything like that. Second, after seeing Jesus, he thought about how his impression of Him had changed. He had expected Him to be a mad man, a man who would be shouting and telling people that the end was near. Dovid had seen false prophets before, but this man looked and acted nothing like them. He reflected on how, when Levi pointed Him out, that Jesus had looked at them and smiled. Dovid remembered how warm His smile appeared. Finally, what had occurred in the Temple was like nothing he had ever seen before. Aside from the anger which Jesus displayed at the people for selling goods in the house of God, he found that everything He said and quoted was correct. He recalled that, even with a legion of Roman soldiers and all the guards that were posted, no one came to arrest this man. Normally, he would have been taken into custody and charged with disorderly conduct, but that did not happen. Even the merchants did not protest.

So what was it about this man that made Him so different, and what put people at ease when they were around Him? Dovid thought about it, and it came to him—*truth*. This man spoke truth, and He comforted people with His kindness. He spoke to, and spent time with people who were forgotten by others. Dovid thought of what had been said about Jesus— He spent time with sinners, prostitutes, and the sick. Why? What did they have to give Him? Would they be the people He would use to start His army when He attempts to take on the Romans? Dovid theorized that could not be. To overthrow the Roman Empire made no sense at all, so why did this man spend time with them? He had no answers, just more questions. Now, he did not want to think anymore. He would deal with this some other time. Right now, he wanted to sit down and spend time with his wife and daughter.

As they prepared the evening meal, Batel asked her daughter to help. As they cooked, she noticed that Dovid was sitting in the corner outside the tent praying with his eyes closed. She thought that was unusual, because he would normally do that with the other men in the community, but this was different. Batel told Eidel to keep working on the meal while she talked to her father. Batel went out and sat by Dovid without speaking. All she could do was to be near him as he prayed, and when he was finished, she would try to determine what was happening. But as she sat, Dovid was in such deep prayer that he did not even hear her sit down. As she listened, she heard him praying for wisdom, patience, and understanding of what was happening in the Holy City. He was so focused on his prayer that he began to recite from Isaiah. Dovid tried to make sense of everything, and tried to get clarification from the Scriptures: *"Everyone who is called by My name, Whom I have created for My glory; I have formed him, yes, I have made him. Before Me there was no God formed, Nor shall there be after Me. I even I, am the Lord, And besides Me there is no savior."* Dovid continued to pray, "Lord help me to understand these words from your Prophet Isaiah, for he spoke the truth you showed him. Lord, I am very confused by what I have seen. Help me to hear your voice again to make sure I have not gone astray." Dovid, with his face bowed down, was speaking to God and asking for a sign, "Lord, please send me a sign to know what you would have me do. I need to hear from you again. As I sit here in the silence, please give me a word or a sign, please Lord, I am at a loss. I do not know what to do. Lord, today, I spoke out in anger to all who were there. Lord, I follow your commandments, and you know all my works and deeds. I seek your comfort Lord. God you have told us that you are the only God. No other exists. How do I accept this man as your Son? Many have come claiming to be the Messiah and have proven to be fake. I am so confused. I do not know what or who to believe. You have told me that your Glory and power would be revealed here in the Holy City, and yet, I do not know how to discern what that will be or who it will be. Father, I pray that you will help me through this time and help me to be understanding and not stiff-necked about what you will reveal to us." Dovid had never prayed like this before.

As he finished praying, he opened his eyes and noticed Batel sitting beside him, and he inquired, "How long have you been there?" She spoke, "Not long. What is troubling you, my husband? You are so tense and on edge. What can I do to ease your burdens?" Dovid explained to Batel that he was concerned about losing the traditions that were established by Abraham and Moses and all the forefathers before them. Dovid told her, "All I see is how people are worried about what the future will be. What will become of us? I tell you that my father and his father never worried about what the future held. They knew that if they feared the Lord, he would lead them to the Promised Land. Today this talk about Jesus being the Christ and everyone talking about where He would lead us is unnerving. Is He taking us in the wrong direction?"

Batel asked, "Dovid, do you not think that this man could be the Messiah? With everything you have experienced this week, maybe this is what God was telling you and Levi—that His Glory and Power would be in this man." Dovid looked at her and spoke, "How could you think this way when you did not see this man? I did. He is no more the Messiah than I am. His look, those with whom He associates, and even the things He does, all go against what the laws of Moses have taught us. Any man who calls himself the Son of God and then eats and spends time with the sinners and then goes to the High

Priests and challenges them, cannot be the Messiah." He gave Batel an angry look as if to say, "Do not question me." He told her, "And, if that is not enough, He heals people on the Sabbath. How could He be the Messiah?"

Batel did not want to get Dovid more upset, so she told him, "I am not trying to question your wisdom or what you have seen. As you say, I have not seen this man, but many people whom are much wiser than I have said He is the Messiah." Now angry, Dovid shouted out, "Who?" She looked away and said, "Well, see I have made you angry. Let us forget it." Now, even angrier he said, "No, tell me just one person who would say this?" His face now red, she answered, "For one, our Rabbi and friend Ishaq." The red face quickly went from red to pale in a matter of seconds. His voice, now softened he tells her, "Yes, that is true, but he was very old. He could not be completely positive." "Dovid, then why did he come to you in the dream? Was that not God's work? You know that God had sent him to you to listen to him." "Yes, yes, I know, but God did not send Ishaq to tell me to follow this man. We do not know the outcome of what God has in store for us here. But, my dear wife, I can tell you this; if this man that everyone has called the Messiah is truly Him, I will be very surprised and will... oh, never mind, He is not the Messiah, that's that. Let us get the children and spend some time with them." "Then why are you so upset?" He replied, "I do not know, I just do not know. I just want to know the truth and live and give our children a good life and follow our God's will."

During the mid-day meal all the conversation around the tent area was about Jesus and that He was going to be in the Temple that afternoon to teach. Levi wanted to be present to hear Him. Azel came by and asked Dovid if he had heard that Jesus was going to be in the Temple preaching. "Do you want to come? Let us hear what He has to say. I want to learn more about this man and who He is." Dovid admonished him, "Be careful what you do and who you spend time around. Before you know it, He will have you fooled like the rest of these people."

Azel sat down and told him, "My old friend, I did not say I was a follower of this man, but He has healed people, and some say He has raised a man from the dead. Now, I do not know about you, but even Moses could not do that." Dovid turned his head away. Looking now at the Temple, he closed his eyes and told his friend, "You go; I have no interest in this man."

"Would you mind if Levi came along? He appeared to have good Scripture knowledge and he would be a great help to me." Dovid now turned around again, "Why? You know the Scriptures." "Yes, but your son has a vast knowledge, and he also seems interested in what this man has to say. I know he wants to go, but is afraid to ask you." "Why would my son be afraid to speak to me?" Azel looked at him and without saying a word, shook his head and got up to leave. Dovid turned to see Levi gazing at the ground as if afraid to even look at his father. Dovid turned and asked Azel, "What is going on here? I am not interested in seeing this man, and I want to make sure that the traditions of our people stay intact. All of a sudden, I am feared. Has everyone lost their minds?" As Azel walked away, Dovid shouted to his friend, "Take Levi with you." Levi picked his head up and looked at his father and with fear, yet anticipation in his eyes, arose slowly. "Are you sure Father?" Dovid nodded his head. Levi hugged his father and kissed his mother and walked off in Azel's direction. Batel looked at her husband and smiled. Dovid shouted out one more time and told Azel to wait a minute. Azel and Levi turned around to see what Dovid wanted, and he told them, "You know, I am not sure this is such a good idea." Levi looked disappointed, but Dovid continued, "I had better come with you so that I can be the voice of reason." Levi, now smiling from ear-to-ear, ran back to his father and hugged him tightly. Dovid whispered to himself, "I do not know what I am doing here. What have I gotten myself into?"

As the men and Levi arrived at the Temple, it was so crowded that they had to make their way through throngs of people just to be able to see Jesus. But as they grew nearer, they heard people questioning Him. Levi, at this point, could only see His hair from behind, because Jesus was being asked a question from the other side of the Temple. In the corner was a group of men, who appeared to be of authority, asking questions. Azel whispered to Dovid, "Do you know who those men are?" Dovid told him, "Yes, they are the Chief Priest and the scribes, together with the elders." Azel looked at Levi with his eyes wide open as if to say, "Wow, this is really special." Then the Chief Priest asked Jesus, *"Tell us by what authority are you doing these things? Or who is he who gave you this authority?"*

Then Dovid confided in Azel and Levi, "That is the question I would like answered too." Dovid, now really listening and hoping to hear what everyone—including the Chief Priest—was hoping Jesus would say. But as Dovid finished speaking to Azel and Levi, Jesus turned to the group and asked them a question, *"Tell me, the baptism of John—was it from heaven or from men?"* Jesus then turned toward the crowd. Just then the Chief Priest and the scribes were huddled together thinking of a response. The crowd now waited to hear the response from this learned group of men. Dovid asked Azel, "Who is John?" Azel told Dovid who he was, and by then one of the scribes had answered Jesus, *"We do not know."*

Dovid and all the others, surprised that this man had stumped the most learned men in Jerusalem, heard Jesus say to them, *"Neither will I tell you by what authority I do these things."* At this, the Chief Priest and the others left the area, and Jesus continued to speak to the people. As He began, the people were now sitting and listening to Him. Levi thought back to the first time he saw Jesus and the feeling that He was talking directly to him. Jesus told them a story, "*A certain man planted a vineyard, leased it to vinedressers, and went into a far country for a long time. Now at vintage time, he sent a servant to the vinedressers that they might give him some of the fruit of the vineyard. But the vinedressers beat him and sent him away empty-handed. Again, he sent another servant; and they beat him also, treated him shamefully, and sent him away empty-handed. And again he sent a third; and they wounded him also and cast him out. Then the owner of the vineyard said, 'What shall I do? I will send my beloved son, probably they will respect him when they see him.' They reasoned among themselves, saying, 'this is the heir. Come; let us kill him, that the inheritance may be ours.' So they cast him out of the vineyard and killed him. Therefore, what will the owner of the vineyard do to them? He will come and destroy those vinedressers and give the vineyard to others.*"

Now Dovid was puzzled by what was just said, and he was thinking to himself, "What is He telling us?" As He finished, He looked directly at Dovid. Dovid felt Jesus' eyes piercing right through him. Dovid felt uneasy, looked away, and then back. Levi, trying to understand what was just said, hung on every word this man said. He thought Jesus was talking about someone from the vineyard close by in the mountains. By now, all the people were confused as to what Jesus was talking about, and just then a man shouted out from behind to Dovid and the others, "*Certainly not!*" Then, everyone turned around and saw that the Chief Priest and the others had not left, that they had been in the back listening to Him preach. Dovid turned and realized that, not only were they present, but Jesus was not looking at him, rather the Chief Priest who was behind him.

Many of the people shook their heads in agreement with the scribe who shouted this out, awaiting Jesus' response.

Now with a loud voice they heard Him say, *"What then is written?"* He then told them about the stone which the builders rejected that had become the chief cornerstone. Levi was now really paying close attention because He was referring to the Scriptures which King David himself had written. Levi became as white as a ghost. Dovid looked at his son and whispered, "What is wrong?" Now for the first time, Levi realized what the story was about. He thought to himself that this man was referring to the Messiah, that God had sent prophets and kings to tell the people about His coming. He sent them to tell of what God desired His people to do, and mankind rejected the messengers. Now He was sending His Son, and they were rejecting Him also. King David prophesized that God would send the Messiah, and He also would be rejected.

Levi looked at his father and whispered, "He is talking about what King David had foretold." Jesus continued speaking, *"That whoever falls on that stone will be broken; but on whomever it falls, it will grind him to powder."*

Dovid glanced at his son and Azel, and then at Jesus, and as he saw Jesus looking in his direction, a wave of panic overcame him. "We need to leave now." "But, Father," Levi said. "He is not finished." "But we are, Levi. We are going now." Dovid pulled him up by his arm and they walked through the crowd as quickly as possible, trying not to step on people as they went. Dovid spoke softly to Levi as he bent over to tell him, "Hurry, we need to hurry." At this point, he was dragging his son behind him by the arm. Once outside the Temple courts, Dovid was having a hard time catching his breath. He was bent over and trying to get air. Levi, also out of breath, was bent over with his hands on his knees as he asked his father, "Why did we have to leave?" Dovid replied, "I do not want you to spend any more time near this man." "Why Father? He is, if nothing else, a prophet. Did you see the way He looks at people? It is almost as if He is talking directly to us." "Levi, did you hear me? No more. I mean it. I do not want Him mentioned anymore."

Levi looked at his father with disbelief. Still bent over, Dovid did not see the anger in his son's face. Levi had always been a good son and knew the importance of respecting his father. Since he had been studying the Scriptures, he knew all too well the commandment that says, *"Honor your father and your mother, that your days may be long upon the land which the Lord your God is giving you."* So his disagreement with his father was only internal. He would never, in his mind, dishonor his parents either verbally or in deed.

After hearing Jesus speak in the Temple, and for the second time speak of the Scriptures, Levi realized that this man was more than just an ordinary man. If nothing else, He was one of the most knowledgeable people he had ever heard speak God's Word. Dovid now caught his breath and looked up at Levi saying, "Let us get back to your mother and sister." Levi asked, "What about Azel? Should we not wait for him?" Dovid told Levi that he could find his way back. "I informed him we were leaving. He can make his own decisions. Levi, we need to leave now."

Levi, not wanting to question his father agreed and turned his head toward the Temple entrance hoping that he would see Azel, but with all the people standing outside, he did not see him. As they walked and were now outside the entrance of the Temple, he heard his father talking to himself, out loud, about what Jesus had spoken earlier. "How can this man call himself the Son of God? He does not even respect the Chief Priests. Are they not from God, and do they not honor the laws of Moses?" Upon hearing this, Levi felt this rage come over him, and he tried to control himself and not say anything to disrespect his father, but Levi needed to make sure his father understood the Scriptures. So, as they were walking side-by-side, Levi stopped abruptly, and Dovid also stopped and turned as he spoke, "What is wrong my son?" "Father, why did we leave so hastily? What happened in there? I do not understand. Did Jesus say something that was not true?" Dovid looked at his son with fire in his eyes and said, "You know the law better than I do. Are you not to honor your father and mother?" "Yes, I am, and I do." Dovid shouted, "No you do not. We will not discuss this anymore. I said, we are leaving, and that is it. I do not have to explain to you my reasons." Dovid began to walk again. Levi, still standing there, just would not move. Dovid turned again, looked at Levi, and said, "I said, let us go now. Son, you are not too old for me to still punish you." "Yes, Father, I know, but in this case, you are wrong." There it was lying out in the open. Levi blurted out his true feelings. Levi tried to control his anger. Everything he had always followed had just come to an abrupt end. He could not take the words back, and now he had done the unexpected—he had dishonored his father. Dovid walked toward his son. He knew he was in big trouble, thinking the worst was about to happen. Levi had never been struck, and had only heard other friends speak of their fathers' punishments. He was about to experience his father's wrath.

Dovid got right up to his son, and Levi placed his head down not knowing what to expect. Dovid told his son, "I am very disappointed with you Levi, and I will not tolerate this kind of disrespect. How dare you talk back to me that way? I know what is best, and I know that what that man spoke in the Temple today was wrong." Levi then looked up at his father and asked, "What did He say that was wrong? He was answering their questions." "Well, He did not answer their question that asked about 'by what authority He does these things.' He insulted the leaders of the Temple. No true man of God would ever do that." "Father, I am not so sure. He did not answer them as much as they did not answer Him." Now angry, Dovid told Levi, "You see you are becoming just like the others. Are you my son and the son of Abraham,

Isaac, and Jacob or not?" "I am, and I believe that this man, Jesus, is also, but we do not know enough yet to say one way or the other if He is the Messiah or not." Dovid's face was once again beat red as he told his son, "Well, I have seen enough to know that He is not. That is the reason you will not see Him again. I do not want Him to distract you from your life's work." Levi then shouted back, telling his father, "I do not know what to believe anymore, but I do know that running away from this will not help us understand what or who this man is." Calming down, Levi became remorseful for shouting at his father.

Dovid realized that the exchange between him and his son had now taken on a new level. Levi had never spoken to his father like this, and his father was surprised by his son's response. Dovid told Levi, "Let us get back to the tent, and we will discuss this when we have both cooled down." Levi looked at his father and agreed as they approached the tents. By this time, Levi was crying because he realized how he had spoken to his father. He stopped once more, and Dovid continued to head toward the tent. Levi realized that his father was not going to stop and talk with him, so Levi continued to the tent by himself, feeling worse than ever.

Neither Dovid nor Levi spoke a word to each other the rest of the evening. Batel talked to both her son and her husband, trying to get them together; however, Dovid did not want to talk with his son. Levi looked for a way to get past what had occurred and apologize. But, when Levi tried to talk, his father held his hand up as if to say, "Please do not talk to me about this. I am very angry right now." So Levi walked away to spend time with his sister. As the evening ended, they all went to bed and Levi prayed that the Lord would forgive him for his sin, and also that his father would also forgive him for the disagreement. As Levi closed his eyes, he could not get Jesus out of his mind. What an impact He had had on Levi. Every time he closed his eyes, he saw Jesus turning toward him as He spoke. Levi, now unable to sleep, looked at the top of the tent thinking to himself; "If this man is God, why are so many people disagreeing with Him? If He is God, why not come down from heaven or disappear and reappear? That would show them, but He does not do anything. He is a normal-looking man and He is not what people expected Him to be like." Still, Levi could not disagree with what He has spoken. "Clearly, He is a prophet." Levi attempted to sleep and continued to go over it in his mind. It took a few moments to think about the stars and the good things he had to be thankful for and what God had spoken to him. As he did so, his eyes closed and he drifted off to sleep.

DAY EIGHT

✝

Now the Passover was only a couple of days away. The time was about 5:00 in the morning and Levi was awakened by a dream. He saw people crying and asking why this had happened. Why would God allow this to happen? Levi did not understand what had happened, so he asked a bystander why everyone was crying. This man looked at Levi and told him that the day of the Lord had come, and they were not ready. God was to bring judgment on His people who did not recognize Him.

Keenly aware of it being morning, but very early, Levi jumped up. He could see that his family was still asleep, and the sun was not even above the horizon yet. So he got up, went outside, and looked to the heavens and asked God in prayer, "*Save me, O God, by your name, and vindicate me by your strength. Hear my prayer, O God. Give ear to the words of my mouth. For I will freely sacrifice to you; I will praise your name, O Lord, for it is good.*" This he spoke from the Psalms. Levi thought to himself, "I know what my father has told me, but I must find out more so that we do not miss the Lord if He comes, especially if this is truly Him." Levi decided to head back to Bethany where Jesus was staying in hopes of seeing Him preach or talk with Him. He headed out toward Bethany by himself.

On route to Bethany, he reached the top of the hill where they had been the day before. This hill was called the Mount of Olives. As he reached the crest of the hill, he noticed a small group of people heading his way. From this distance, he could not tell who they were, but as he moved closer, they became clearer. Yes, Jesus and His followers were headed his way, only the large crowds were no longer with Him. As he reached the group, he looked at Jesus, and Jesus and the disciples looked at him and greeted him with a smile and a well wish for a good day. Perhaps it was too early, but the few that followed Him included the woman he had met just the other day. "Good morning, my child! How are you today, and where is your friend?" "I am by myself today," Levi explained. "Why do you look so unhappy? Are you not feeling well?" Levi began to explain what had happened the previous day and realized that he was telling things he was feeling to a strange woman, and he did not understand why. "Well, you are blessed to be in the presence of the Lord my child. Be well and follow His ways. He has come to free all the people." Levi then followed them toward Jerusalem. He was very close to them now and could hear what was being said.

As they reached the top of the hill, one of Jesus' disciples remarked to Jesus that the tree that He had cursed the day before was now dead. Then Jesus said to them all, "*Have faith in God, I tell you the truth, if anyone says to this mountain, go throw yourself into the sea, and does not doubt in his heart, but believes that what he says will happen, it will be done for him. Therefore I tell you, whatever you ask for in prayer, believe that you have received it, and it will be yours.*" As He said this, Levi looked toward the fortress of King Herod, where the sun was rising and casting a shadow on the mountain. Levi noticed that as Jesus said these words, the sun was rising from the east and coming up from behind Him. As it shown on Him it made a spectacular sight! Levi was moved by what Jesus said, along with the bigger-than-life shadow that it made of Him. As He raised His hands in the air and spoke to the group, the shadow made Him appear to be in the shape of an angel. As they traveled along, many people came up to Jesus to ask Him questions, others requested blessings, and yet others requested healing. Some of the people asking Him questions were scribes or Pharisees.

Levi was interested in what was being asked. Levi, knowing the Scriptures well, hoped to hear how He would answer. One of the Pharisees asked Jesus, *"Tell us, therefore, what do you think? Is it lawful to pay taxes to Caesar, or not?"* Looking directly at these men, Jesus stopped now and said, *"Why do you test me, you hypocrites?"* Then Jesus asked them to show Him the money and after looking at it, He asked them a question, *"Who is on the coin?"* They replied, *"Caesar."* He told them to give to Caesar that which was his and to God that which was God's. Stunned at His answer, they looked at each other and immediately walked away. As they arrived into the city and came to the entrance of the Temple, the Pharisees stopped Him again, but before they could ask Him a question, He asked them one. Jesus asked the group of Pharisees, *"What do you think about the Christ? Whose Son is He?"* The group said to Him, *"The son of David."* Then Jesus looked at them and said, *"If that is true, how does David in the spirit call Him Lord, saying, 'The Lord said to my Lord. Sit at My right hand until I make your enemies your footstool.'"* Puzzled by this, Levi realized that he did not know either. With that, Levi got the chills, his whole body shook, and he was so overwhelmed with what Jesus said, that he thought to himself that this man must either be the Messiah or the craziest man to ever live!

The Pharisees were now outsmarted and could not answer Him. The Pharisees were visibly angry. The people around them were now saying, "This is truly the Messiah. We have our King, all Praise and Honor be yours now and forever." Levi watched the most learned men of the law walk away in silence. Levi felt a hand on his shoulder. In a panic, he turned around to see who it was, and noticed it was the woman who was with them. She looked at Levi and said, "Has what the Lord said moved you?" Levi could not speak; he just shook his head in affirmation. Then he spoke to her from the prophet Isaiah, *"I even I, am He who comforts you. Who are you that you should be afraid?"* As he said this, Jesus hearing it looked at Levi and said, "You speak the truth." Levi now realizing that he was in the presence of Jesus, looked down as if he were not worthy to even speak to this man. Then one of His disciples placed his arm on Levi's shoulder and said, "Child what is your name?" Levi looked at the man, and with his hands shaking and having little saliva to speak, barely got his name out. "Levi." The disciple smiled and told him that he had a strong name meaning lion. "So tell me Levi, are you the lion of your family's heritage?" Levi, answering the question, told them, "Yes, I believe so." "Have we seen you before?" Another disciple answered, "Yes, we have seen him before. He is the young man that got knocked over the other day, and the teacher picked him up." They all laughed, and Levi asked, "Sir, if I may, what is your name?" He looked at Levi and said, "My name is Phillip." Levi backed away and told them, "I must be getting back to my family." Then another one of the disciples spoke out to Levi, "Peace be with you." Levi backed away and ran back to the tent area.

As Levi made his way back, he was haunted by what he had just seen and heard. He had seen Jesus speak the Scriptures as if He had written them. He had seen the Pharisees stumped by the word of this man, and he had been in the direct presence and been affirmed by Jesus, who told Levi he spoke the truth.

Ever since they began their pilgrimage to Jerusalem, Levi's goal of seeing and hearing this man seemed so unbelievable. Now he had seen Him and listened to Him preach, and been in His presence as He spoke and rebuked the Pharisees. In all his studies, he had never been so moved as he had been these last few days in the presence of Jesus. As Levi approached the tent area, his entire jubilee vanished as he realized that he had to face his father and mother and explain where he had been. Never before having disobeyed them, he was now faced with the prospect of telling his parents why he felt it was important for him to go and see Jesus again.

Upon reaching the tent about 7:30 in the morning, many people were already up and moving about. As Levi walked past the people, many of them were busy preparing breakfast. Some of the people who saw him, did not look directly at him. This made Levi feel very uncomfortable; he quickly realized that something was wrong. As he stood outside his tent, he noticed that the family was not outside. He bent over and walked in, waiting to hear from his parents regarding their anger. He noticed they were busy getting things together so that they could all go into the town today. Batel was the first to ask him, "Levi, we have been waiting for you. Did you enjoy your walk? Did it help to clear your head? I told your father when he awoke that you had gone for a walk." Levi, looking puzzled, stumbled over his words and without looking at his father muttered, "Oh, oh, yes I... did. Yes, many things were revealed to me. Let me help you with that mother. It appears to be heavy." Levi's mother gave him a look as if to say, "I know where you were."

Dovid came over and placed his arm on his son's shoulder as he bent over to pick up some of the blankets they used from the previous night. Levi stood up and turned to look at his father, worried that by now, he knew where he had been and would call him on it. Levi, not saying anything, turned and waited for his father to confront him, but instead Dovid asked Levi, "Is anything wrong? You are very quiet this morning." "No Father, everything is fine." "Levi, I know we did not talk much last night, and I want us to clear the air about what happened so that you understand why I feel the way I do, and why I am concerned for you." Levi told his father, "There is no need to discuss it. I understand your feelings, and I am sorry for disagreeing with you in public. Father, I know you do not understand why Jesus did what He did, and I know it frightened you to the point of your needing to walk out. Believe me, I felt that way too, but I know that we are under God's wing and protection as it is written by King David that, '*Surely He shall deliver you from the snare of the fowler and from the perilous pestilence. He shall cover you with His feathers, and under His wings you shall take refuge; His truth shall be your shield and buckler.*' If we know this to be true Father, why do you worry that this man is evil? Would not God himself cover us and protect us from such?" Dovid told his son, "You are wise beyond your years with the understanding of the Scriptures, but on this matter, you are just a child and I am telling you, you must stay away from this man." Levi, not wanting to confront his father, did not debate the topic any further.

Levi was, however, confronted by his mother. Batel was a quiet woman who understood that Dovid was the head of the household. Not once had she ever misled her husband. This day she covered for her son because she knew that tensions were high between Dovid and Levi, and she desired them to reconcile. She had always been the peacemaker in the family, but could be tough when she needed to be. This was one of those occasions. As Dovid walked away, she walked over to Levi who was doing some chores and questioned him saying, "Why did you leave this morning and not tell us where you were going? You have never done anything like that before. Why would you do that?" Levi was not accustomed to lying or to being questioned on his actions. He had always been obedient to his parents and others. So when his mother questioned him on where he had gone, he wanted to tell her, but was afraid that if he did, she would become very upset. He elected to not say anything, so she asked him again, "Levi, where did you go? Were you out seeking this man, Jesus, again?" He looked at her, and wanting to obey his mother, did not lie, but answered in the affirmative. Her face paled as she asked him, "Why?" In a whisper, she asked, "Why would you disobey your father's wishes? I do not understand what is so alluring about this man. I will tell you this, if your father hears about this from someone other than you, his heart will be broken." Levi, concerned with what his mother had just said and the guilt he felt about not telling them where he had been, was almost more than he could bear. Levi retorted, "Mother, you know father would not understand. I have tried to talk to him about it, but every time I do, he cuts me off and tells me he will not discuss this man with me again. When we were in the Temple yesterday and heard Jesus speak, I was so moved, along with all who heard Him. I have never heard anyone speak like this before. Mother, you know how I have always admired Ishaq and what he taught me, but this man teaches with such passion and understanding. It is as though He wrote the Torah."

At this, Batel said to her son, "I understand that He is a very good teacher, but your father is a wise man, and if he says this man is not the Messiah, why do you question him?" Levi, trying to be understanding of what his mother's concerns were, replied, "Mother, you do not understand. I saw Him. I have been near Him, and it is like nothing I have ever seen or heard. Father himself, at hearing this man, was moved to tears, but then pulled me by the arm and ran out of the Temple. By the time we stopped we were both winded. I have never seen him afraid before, but he was visibly shaken. When I asked him why, he just ignored me. He commented that we needed to leave because we had to get back here. I wish you could hear Jesus speak and see Him. Then, you would know what I feel and why I need to hear more of Him to make sure I am not crazy." "Levi, you must under-stand—I will not do anything to go against your father. I have heard much about this man, and I can see from your passion that you have been captured by His charisma, but you must obey your father's wishes." Levi, now distraught at his mother's statement, returned to doing his chores and knew that he must obey his parent's wishes. As he began his chores, he prayed to God for His help in his family's under-standing of his wishes and asked God for His intervention with his father.

Batel realized that her son's passion for the Scriptures was strong and that his understanding was far beyond hers or that of her husband's. She also wanted peace in the home and knew that both her husband and son were made from the same cloth of stubbornness. She was not sure what to believe, and she knew that she would like to meet this man and see what He was all about. The only glimpse she had gotten of Him was when He passed by the tent area a few days ago, and she really was too far away to see Him. However, she was impressed by the crowd and the number of people who followed Him. Besides, all the women who had done nothing but talk about the miracles and acts of kindness He had done, had left an impression upon her, but she needed to make sure that the family harmony and peace stayed in place. She believed her job was to keep unity in the family, and at the same time, honor God's commands. Yet, in the back of her mind she thought about her husband's dream, and how they had both been visited by their old friend Ishaq, who foretold what God had in store for them this Passover season. Could all of this be tied together, and if so, why? She would have to think on how to get them to talk again and bridge the gap in their understanding of what God's mission was for them, and doing so was urgent here this week, right now!

Levi, on the other hand, was thinking about what he could say to his father. He knew that whatever he told him must be well thought out. The one thing he did not want was to lose his composure as before, whereby disobeying his father and, at the same time, further eliminating the possibility of open dialogue. As Levi waited all day to speak to his father, he thought long and hard about what to say, realizing that the only thing to do was to be honest and say what he had done and why he did it.

By this time, the burden of telling his father where he had been that morning was weighing heavy on him. The longer he waited, the more difficult it became. The agonizing was so severe that he was experiencing stomach problems, and he had talked himself out of telling his father three times already. The hour was getting late, and it was almost time to turn in, but Levi was still pacing around the area. Dovid asked Levi, "Why are you pacing so much and what is it you need to tell me?" Levi thought to himself, "I just need to tell him here and now, so here goes." Levi walked up to his father and took a deep breath, announcing, "Father, I need to tell you something." "What is it my son?" Levi tried to tell him, but the words were like stumbling blocks—the more he tried to explain, the worse it got. At this, Dovid could tell his son was struggling, so he announced, "I have been waiting for you to come and tell me what is on your mind. I could see all day that you were struggling with something. You know, my son, you are very easy to read. You carry your burdens around on your shoulders where everyone can see them. I was wondering when you would come to me and tell me what I already know." Levi looked up at his father and asked, "You were?" "Yes, so speak what is in your heart." Levi smiled at his father and told him, "You are correct father! What I wanted to tell you is... is um..., well, you see..." Dovid then interrupted and said, "You wanted to tell me you are sorry for being disrespectful, do you not?" Levi answered, "Well, yes this is true..." Levi agreed with his father, but more needed to be said; however, the words were not forthcoming. So, instead of telling him what really happened, Levi just shook his head, yes, and said, "Thank you for understanding. I am truly sorry." "My son, I love you with all my heart. You are forgiven, but please, no more of these madman stories. We are to obey God and God only— none of this nonsense of healing and raising the dead. Let us not be at odds any longer." With that, Dovid placed his arms around his son and kissed him on both cheeks. As Dovid released Levi, but still held onto his shoulders, he added, "Let us ask for God's forgiveness and reconciliation." As he looked up at his father, he could not disagree again, so Levi agreed by nodding his head.

As Levi finished talking to his father, he ran back in the tent right past his mother who smiled at him, while noticing that he had his head down and looked upset. She looked at Dovid and asked, "What did you say to Levi?" Dovid, smiling, told her what happened. She realized that her son had not been totally truthful with his father. Batel went in to talk to Levi and asked, "Are you okay, my son?" Levi nodded, "Yes." But, she knew better. He was unhappy and upset because he could not disobey his father again, and that he had been unable to tell his father what he believed. As she knelt and placed her head on his shoulder, she whispered with tears in her eyes, "My child, be strong in the Lord! Be strong in the Lord!" Realizing that this was not going to get better, she had to think of something she could do to help her son and her husband.

As everyone retired for the night, she lay awake praying to God to give her the strength and insight to help her family, and to know what to believe and follow for herself. She was torn as she agonized, "I do not know what to do. To whom

should I listen? I pray that I will have the correct answers."
As she sat in the dark, she struggled with how to facilitate
communication between her husband and her son. She was
trying to find a way to bridge that gap. What could she do?
How could she get them talking? All the lanterns had been
turned off, and the sky was overcast so that no natural light
emitted from the moon, creating a pitch-black effect. She
could not even see to the end of the tent. She could not sleep
and could not arise. So, in the deep, dark part of the night,
all she could do was close her eyes and attempt to sleep.
As she lay awake she realized that the best way to support
her family was to go into town and see this man for herself;
to witness personally what He was all about. She did not
desire to take sides, but she knew that her husband and son
were heading for deep problems. She came up with an idea
to solve this problem, and as she did, a smile broke across
her face in the dark. She thanked God and closed her eyes
again as she finally fell asleep.

DAY NINE

✝

As the day began, Batel arose early and Dovid noticed that her whole demeanor was different. She was singing songs of praise and she had an unusual smile on her face. Dovid asked, "My wife, why are you so happy this day?" She replied, "Nothing specific; I am blessed by our God and loved by my family. Maybe it is the anticipation of the Passover and what the harvest will bring this year." Dovid smiled at her and said, "Whatever the reason that you are happy is reason for me to be joyful. I am blessed by your smile this morning." She acknowledged his kindness by giving him a kiss on the cheek and whispered to herself, "You have no idea."

As both Batel and Dovid were enjoying each others' company, Levi and Eidel came outside. As they did, Eidel, smiling, but still not quite awake, went over to her father and hugged him, but Levi did not look very happy. He was still struggling from the night before. Avoiding his father, he would not even look at him. As his mother observed his unhappiness, she said to him, "Good morning, my child. Is something wrong?" He looked up and quietly said, "I am not feeling well. My stomach has been upset since I woke up today." Batel put her arms around him and kissed him on the forehead to see if he was warm; he was not. She smiled and reassured him, "I believe you are going to feel better soon. Let us eat and see what the Lord will have us do this glorious day." As they began to eat, Dovid asked Levi if he would like to help him get the lamb prepared for the Passover dinner. Levi, not even looking at his father, said, "I will do whatever you ask." This was not exactly the response for which his father was searching. "Levi, do you not want to help prepare for the meal?" "Yes, I do. I am just not feeling well today." Dovid looked at Batel as if to say, "What is the matter?" Batel, now looking at her husband, said, "Perhaps we should finish eating and go into town. I have some things I still need before I have everything for the meal." Dovid told Batel, "Levi and I can go for you if you wish." "No, I think I would like to go myself. Levi can go with me to carry the supplies. Levi, would you please go with me to help me?" Levi looked at his mother and shook his head, yes. Dovid, now upset that his wife would want to go alone without him, told her, "My dear, I will come along. Traveling to the city at this time of the year can be very dangerous and I am concerned for your safety." "My husband, do not worry. Levi can take care of me and nothing will happen. Besides, Levi and I need to spend some time together. He is almost grown and soon he will be gone." "Very well, but stay away from the Temple area and whatever happens, do not go near that man, Jesus." Batel, now glancing at Levi, said to her husband, "You do not think I can make up my own mind on these matters?" Levi was torn as to why he possessed such a strong desire to see Jesus when he knew it went against his father's will. Looking at his mother, Levi realized for the first time that his trip was more than just a trip to pick up supplies. The trip was planned as an excuse so that his mother might encounter Jesus and learn more about Him firsthand. Levi thought, "I knew she would understand eventually." Then Levi became more alert, and his spirit began mending. He asked his mother if he could have more to eat. He desired not to waste anything. She smiled and said, "Of course."

Later they headed into town toward the merchants' area where Levi and Dovid had encountered Jesus a few days before. The trip into town was filled with Batel's questions of her son's thoughts on this man and why he felt that He could be the Messiah. Batel wanted to be very clear that she was there to see and not to judge who this man was. Levi, now excited to explain what the Scriptures say about His coming and what the times would be like, explained about all the miracles Jesus had done, the specific Scriptures He spoke in the Temple, and the very specific event that occurred the first day they arrived in the Holy City. He explained that when he and Azel had gone out to see Jesus, He arrived in town riding on a donkey which fulfilled the Scripture written by Isaiah.

Batel could see the passion in her son's eyes, the energy with which he spoke, and the excitement in his face. Batel, knowing her son better than anyone, knew this man had had a profound effect on her son. Batel questioned Levi, "Tell me, how is it that if He is the Messiah, and we know that He was sent by God, that He is not recognized by all?" Levi, although very intelligent, could not answer his mother's question. All he could say was, "I do not know yet why this is, but I do know this—He speaks like no Rabbi I have ever heard. He knows the Scriptures better than anyone to whom I have ever listened." "Well, maybe we will have the opportunity to see Him today, and I can see this man for myself." As they continued to head toward the shops, they walked in silence. As they walked, Batel prayed that God would give them the opportunity to see Him, and then she could see what was so special about Him but, she also knew that this was a very difficult situation because she did not want to go against her husband's wishes for her son.

When they arrived at the shopping area, they were waiting in line, and as they did so, several men stood in the corner discussing what Jesus was doing. They were arguing amongst themselves about what should be done. Levi recognized one of the men as one who had been questioning Jesus in the Temple. Realizing he was a Pharisee, Levi paid close attention to the conversation. As they continued, they discussed how they would get rid of Jesus. They discussed different ways. One rationalized that perhaps they could find Him guilty of blasphemy and could have Him stoned. Another suggested that perhaps they could kidnap Him and take Him outside of town; however, one of the men indicated that this would be difficult because of all the people who were always surrounding Him, making it risky and nearly impossible. As they continued the discussion another Priest interjected, "Perhaps, we should just pay someone to kill Him." At this, one of the scribes jumped up and exclaimed, "We cannot do that! It would be unholy for us to participate in that. No, we must trick the Romans into helping us get rid of this man before He creates riots," "Yes," the other Priest concurred, "You are correct. If the Romans can get rid of Him for us, that would be the best thing that could happen! If we can fabricate some charge against Him, we can coerce Pontius Pilot to put Him to death. But how do we get to Him? The crowds are so large that it would be next to impossible to reach Him." "Yes, you are correct! Perhaps we can persuade one of His disciples to bring Him to us." They theorized that these men were poor fishermen, and one of them could be persuaded to give Him up. "That is our opportunity—if we can only find one of them to tell us where He is at night, we can arrest Him, and no one will ever know. We must get rid of Him. He is getting people to believe these stories and healings. More importantly, He is making us look foolish in front of the people."

As Levi and his mother overheard this, a look of panic crossed Levi's face! He whispered to his mother that they were going to kill Jesus. Batel agreed with her son, but told him not to mention it for now. They did not want any problems, for fear they might arrest Levi as well. Upon finishing their shopping, Levi was thinking about what he had overheard and was concerned with how he could warn Jesus. As they headed back toward the tent area, his mother turned to him and said, "Levi, maybe since we are here, we should go into the Temple to pray for a while. Would you like to do that?" Levi's dark eyes lit up, and an expression of gratefulness covered his face. "Maybe we will see Jesus there Mother, and you can hear Him speak." "Levi, remember what your father told you! We do not want to disobey him." "Yes, I know." "Maybe we should just leave then." Levi replied, "No, we should never miss the opportunity to pray. Besides, I am asking you to take me to the Temple for prayer, so let us go."

Upon reaching the Temple, it was quiet. As they went in to pray, Levi quickly searched the grounds to see if Jesus was there. He looked around in a circle and then up and down the corridors to see if he could find Him. He did not see Him. Batel motioned to Levi to come so they could pray. Shortly afterwards as they were making their way back to the tent area, they traveled from the western exit of the Temple, which took them toward the pool of Siloam. They approached the pool of Siloam, and heard a commotion. People were shouting! A large crowd had gathered! They really could not tell what was happening. As they approached, they realized that Jesus was being questioned by the people, and some were people they had seen earlier who were now shouting questions at Him. One yelled out, "How dare you place yourself on equal ground with the God of our Fathers? What gives you the right to do and say these things?" Levi and Batel tried to inch their way closer to hear better, and Batel so desired to get a glimpse of this man. Her heart was racing, not just from the shouting, but with the anticipation of seeing this man for the first time.

Levi heard shouting from behind him. He turned to see and noticed that the crowd was very large. Many of the people were yelling, "Leave Him alone! He is the Messiah!" Others were yelling across that this man was the devil. Batel and Levi were being pushed around by the crowd, and the situation grew more hostile by the minute. Jesus just stood there, not saying anything, just listening to what was being said about Him. One group yelled out, "You are a fake—a blasphemer! You call yourself the Son of God, the Christ, we call you a deceiver of the people." The others were then saying, "You are going to be struck down and killed by God for your wicked ways. You do evil in the sight of the Messiah. May God have pity on your soul!" As these barbs were exchanged back and forth, Levi noticed that they no longer were addressing their comments to Jesus, but now to each other. Levi thought to himself, "How interesting. Was this man not the reason they were fighting? Yet, their passion was not about Him; it was about them being right and the others being wrong."

Now the crowd was beginning to shout, "Let us take Him and kill Him for being a blaspheming liar!" Others were shouting back, "We will kill you before you touch this man." As Levi turned back to look as the crowd pushed him toward the middle, Jesus was gone. The crowd did not even notice that He was not present. Where had He gone? Only after one of His followers announced that He was gone did the crowd realize that He was missing, and they began to disperse. As they moved away from the pools, Batel and Levi noticed that many of the people were divided by what had happened. Many friends, who had been close for so long, were now separated by this man's statements. Batel contemplated, "How can one man divide so many people? How could this man, who divides the people, be the Messiah. If He is God, He should be uniting the people, not dividing them." She reflected that she had never seen such passion by the

people before. How could one man create this much controversy? Yet, even in one's own home, separation can occur.
She inquired of Levi whether or not he was okay. He shook
his head and replied, "Yes, I am fine." "Levi, to where do
you think He disappeared? How could He have gotten away
without anyone noticing?" "I do not know how He got away.
I am just glad He did." Levi then asked his mother the question that cut right to her heart. "Why do so many people hate
Him? I mean, why are they so angry with Jesus?" She was
wondering the same thing, but did not offer up any answers
for her son. Instead, she now questioned her son saying,
"Levi, how do you think God will restore His people to their
rightful place?"

Levi offered up this answer, "What if God has sent this
man to lead us as many of the people said today? What if He
is the one and what if He gets mad and goes back? We will
be wandering for another forty years." "Levi, are you saying
that you believe that this man is the Messiah?" Levi did not
answer at first. In fact, he did not say anything. Instead, he
picked up a rock and threw it. Then, he threw another quietly,
while thinking about how he should respond. He picked up
another, and as he threw it, he told his mother in a very low
voice, "Yes, I do." "Levi, did you say something? I could not
hear you." Levi then told her again, "Yes, I do believe that
this man is who He says He is, which is *the Christ!*"

"How do you know? I mean, how can you be sure?" Levi
then quoted his mother the words of the prophet Isaiah and
the words of King David, along with the words of Daniel
the prophet. "*All of His works have been foretold, and the
prophecy made that He would be known to those who would
be His witnesses in His day.* Consider what we have just
witnessed. The people were shouting at each other for their
beliefs. Did He say that the God of our forefathers was not
the same God? Did He not quote the Scriptures that we have
all read many times and spoke them accurately?" His mother

responded, "Yes." "Then, why do they persecute Him? Why do they want to put Him to death?" "I do not know," Batel responded. "Well, neither do I, Mother, but I do know this—He speaks the Word of God better than anyone I have ever heard, and I feel that deep in my soul He is the Messiah for whom we have waited so long."

Batel, now thought to herself, "How do I know for myself this is true? Dovid does not believe, and yet my son, who is very knowledgeable, speaks from his heart and his understanding of the Scriptures." She had no answers yet. "Which path should I follow?" The walk grew quiet, with neither mother nor son having much to say. As they traveled, Levi looked out across the Kidron Valley and was mesmerized by its beauty and the way the sunshine hit the mountains. The shadow the sun cast on the hillside by the cloud formations was breathtaking.

As they continued in silence, a man came up behind them and startled them to the point that Batel yelled out from the fear. As he spoke, he asked them, "Have you heard the good news?" Levi questioned the man saying, "What good news is this of which you speak?" "God will deliver His people from bondage, and His power and mercy will be revealed in the City of David as He foretold for this season, the season of Jubilee." He continued to speak to them as they traveled, saying, *"How beautiful upon the mountains are the feet of Him who brings good news, who proclaims peace, who brings glad tidings of good things, who proclaims salvation, who says to Zion, your God reigns! Your watchmen shall lift up their voices. With their voices they shall sing together, for they shall see eye-to-eye when the Lord brings back Zion."*

At this declaration, they both turned to look at this man who spoke about God with such elegant beauty, but as they looked at him, his face was covered by the shawl, and the shadow of the sun made it impossible to see him clearly. Batel asked him, "Sir, are you a prophet?" Levi responded, "He is surely a man of God." The man did not answer, but walked ahead, and as he did, the dust of his sandals kicked up dirt into their clothing. Levi recognized His sandals, and as he did so, he stopped and fell to the ground. Batel turned to her son and asked, "Why are you on the ground? Is it because of this man's testimony?" Levi spoke to her and said, "It is Jesus who spoke to us." She turned toward the man walking, and He, now several paces ahead, spoke to Batel, "Your home is blessed by your son's wisdom." She looked at the man's back and thought, "How could I hear Him so clearly? His back is to me, and He is now far away." Batel then turned quickly toward Levi and saw him still on the ground and asked Levi, "Did you hear that?" Levi arose and told his mother, "I did not hear anything." Batel then heard His voice speak to her once again, "Woman, did you find what you were seeking this day?" Stunned, Batel turned toward the man again, but He was gone. "Levi!" she exclaimed, "Where did He go? Levi, He is gone." "Yes, Mother, I can see that. Did I not tell you that He was a man of God—the Messiah—the one for whom we have been waiting?"

Now overwhelmed, Batel was shaking, her heart was racing, and she was filled with excitement, yet concern. She thought, "How could this man be the Messiah? What am I to believe, and more importantly, how do I explain what just happened to Dovid?" For the first time in her life, she was faced with questions that required answers. How was she to go against her husband's wishes? Her fears seemed to be overshadowed by the excitement of her brief encounter with Jesus. She could not believe herself—after just one chance opportunity to meet this man, she was thinking of changing everything she believed up until this point. Batel thought to herself, "What is making me so certain that He is the Messiah? Why do I feel this way? I feel like a little girl again, all excited. My heart is racing like the first time I met my husband; just remembering how my father and Dovid's father arranged for us to meet, but this is more than that. How can I leave everything my parents, husband, and community have taught me, and follow this man's beliefs? He has healed people: the blind, deaf and crippled. He has even raised the dead! That, in itself, should be enough! However, I really did not see Him do any of this, so how do I know it is real? I do not." She thought to herself, "But many people have, so why do I question my thinking?" Batel was growing angry with herself and was wavering back and forth about what to believe. Levi then sensed his mother was wrestling with her thoughts about what she had seen. Levi spoke to her, "I can see you are having a difficult time with everything you have seen, and having Him walk with us on the road and talk directly to you has you confused. Does it not?" Batel did not answer the question, but just thought more about what she had seen. Levi continued to tell her about what the Scriptures say. By quoting Moses, Isaiah, and even King David, he related what the Messiah would say and do, and said that he had fulfilled many of these prophecies, including what he had spoken to them on the road that day. Batel's real concern was the fear of the unknown; what might happen if what she believed was more frightening to her, than what would happen if she did not?

Levi tried to convince his mother with his words, "When I first listened to Him speak, I was amazed by His knowledge and understanding of the Scriptures. I have never heard anyone respond the way He did. Then, like you, I struggled with what to believe, and I've gone back and forth as to who He is and what He has done. Even though I have seen Him a few more times than you, Mother, I truly understand your doubts and have them also. I think the best thing for you to do is to listen to your own heart and make up your own mind, trusting that God will lead you to the truth. Let us concern ourselves with what we know to be true, evaluate what we have seen, and take some time to continue to follow this man so that we have a clear understanding of our thoughts."

Batel looked at her son and spoke, "Well, Levi, one thing I know for sure is that He is a smart man for recognizing your understanding of the Scriptures and that you are a blessing to our family. I thank God everyday for you." Batel thought that maybe this is what God was telling them as they made their way on the journey; maybe this is what Ishaq meant in the dream to Dovid. "Oh, Dovid; what will I tell him and how will I explain everything? Why has God chosen us for this knowledge? We are not of royalty; we are simple, humble working people."

When Batel and Levi returned, Dovid told Batel, "I am glad you are back. I was worried about the two of you. Why are you so late? I was getting ready to look for you." Batel told her husband about the trip, but left out the part of the *encounter*. Batel could not explain it to Dovid when she did not quite understand it yet.

Dovid asked Batel, "Why are you so quiet? I can tell something is wrong. Is something bothering you?" Batel, still not sure how to answer him, told Dovid, "Everything is okay." Levi walked over just a few minutes later, and Dovid asked him, "Did you have a good day my son?" "Yes, Father, I did. Thank you." "And what about your mother? Did anything happen, because she looks like something is bothering her?" Levi looked away and said, "What do you mean?" "What happened in the city that would make your mother so quiet and you not want to tell me what happened?" Levi, not wanting to lie and not wanting to get his mother in trouble, hesitated to respond. Now, Dovid, more suspicious, asked Levi again, "So what happened?" At this point, Batel heard Dovid questioning Levi, and she walked over to intercede. Levi looked at his mother and began to tell his father about the trip. He told his father all about the shopping, and how on the road back, they took a detour to the

Pools of Siloam where they encountered Jesus. Levi paused. Dovid took a deep breath and instructed Levi to continue. Batel wanted him to stop there, but Dovid told his wife, "Let the boy finish. Go on Levi, I am listening." Levi continued, "Well, as we headed back on the road, a man came up behind us. We did not know who He was, but He began to tell us about what was happening in the city and then spoke from the prophet Isaiah." At this point, Batel jumped in and tried to tell Dovid about what happened, but as she did, he raised his hand as if to say, "Stop speaking," and looked at Levi. With a red face, he said, "I told you, I forbid you to see this man any longer, and you once again disobeyed me. After all...." Batel cut her husband off and shouted, "It is my fault!" Dovid turned his head slowly toward his wife, yet his body was still facing his son. She told Dovid, "I wanted to see Him for myself. I wanted to know and hear Him, so I could judge for myself what the other women were talking about. They have seen Him and listened to Him. I wanted to know for myself what this was all about. If you want to be angry, be angry with me."

Dovid did not know what to say. The look of disappointment on his face was clear. After a moment or two, his only comment to his wife was, "Why?" Batel did not answer him. The only thing she said was, "I have to get the meal ready, so please excuse me." She walked away. Dovid was not ready for this conversation to be over, so he followed her as she walked back into the tent. He insisted on an answer. He continued to question her. At this point, Eidel heard them arguing and began to cry. Levi picked her up and told her not to cry, "It is going to be okay." Dovid was still angry and reminded them that he was the head of the family, and that he would not tolerate this kind of behavior. He reminded them that the man of the house had led his family for generations and that was not going to change now. He asked, "Is everyone blind but me? Can you not see that this man is breaking up families, not bringing them together?"

Batel, trying to calm Dovid down, assured him that he was still in charge. She further told him how it happened by chance that they ran into Jesus. Levi waited until his mother was finished, and then attempted to explain to his father that Jesus had told them things that were very specific to them personally. "Levi, many good teachers and Rabbis can speak the Word of God; why even you can do that my son. Levi, does knowing the Word of God as well as many others, make you the Messiah?" Levi shook his head, no. "Then, neither does this make Him the Messiah!" "Yes, Father, but this was different. It was as if He wrote the words Himself, like these were His words." "Levi, that is enough. I will not tolerate this any longer. Do you know what you are saying? You are putting a wedge between this entire family with your disrespect for our family and the laws of our people."

Dovid reminded his son, "The traditions of our people have been a way of life for centuries. Moses was very specific on what God expected from us, and when he came down from the mount, he gave us God's laws. We have since then followed them without exception. The law was made, and because we followed the law, the Lord led us out of captivity. This is the reason we celebrate the Holy Week. Let us not forget the Passover. God will, in His time, tell us when the Messiah will come, but I can assure you it is not this man."

Levi, now horrified at what his father had said, shouted, "Well, you were not there! You did not see or hear Him! I believe that He is who He claims to be! God has revealed it to me in His words and in His miracles!" Batel gasped out loud! Levi turned to look at her, then back to his father. Levi, now stunned that he said it out loud, could not believe that his words and his thoughts came out the way they did. Levi thought to himself, "What did I just do? How could I say that to my father? Why did I not just keep my mouth shut?" Dovid looked at his son and then to his wife as if to say, "Did you just hear what I heard?" Turning back to Levi, Dovid asked him in a very calm manner, "Do you really believe this man is God?"

Levi had spoken honestly about what he believed, and realized this would not sit well with his father. Dovid shook his head as he looked down at the ground, and then up to the heavens as he shouted out loud, "God in heaven, I do not know what I did wrong. Why should I be punished with a son who is disrespectful to me, but more importantly to you God? Please forgive us." As he finished, he walked away in silence toward Azel's tent.

Batel shouted at him, "Dovid, do not go. It will be okay." But he went quietly without saying a word or even a backward glance. As Batel turned to go back inside the tent, Eidel asked her mother why Levi wanted to hurt their father. Levi quickly turned to his sister and then to his mother, awaiting her answer. Batel tried to explain it to her daughter by telling her, "Levi has a belief — what he said, he truly believes. When you believe something with all your heart, you should never be dishonest to yourself or to God. What Levi did was very brave, and he was not trying to hurt your father. Levi was trying to respect what your father has always told him about speaking the truth." Levi now had tears streaming down his face because he realized that, for the first time, he would be an outsider from the family. He knew that his father could not allow this disobedience in his home; the law was clear and must be obeyed.

Levi then ran away. Batel was left alone to comfort her daughter and deal with the guilt in her own mind that somehow she was responsible for this turn of events, because if she had not taken Levi with her, somehow this would never have happened. As she held her child, she could not help but feel the heaviness of this burden that had been placed upon her.

That evening, both Dovid and Levi returned to the tent, but neither spoke to the other, nor to anyone else. They were not hungry and did not even acknowledge that the other existed. This made it a difficult evening and the tension between them was so high that you could almost cut the air with a knife. At the end of the meal, of which little was eaten, prayers were offered for forgiveness of sins and peace upon the people of Israel.

Dovid could not rest and sleep did not come this night, so he arose and went for a walk. The evening was very cold once again, so he put on his outer garments and headed out to clear his head, hoping to get some kind of understanding as to what to do. As he walked, Dovid looked up to the heavens and was struck by how many stars he could see in the night sky. He thought, "If God can create the heavens, surely He can solve this problem for me." As he walked, he noticed that Azel, his friend, was up also, so he walked over to talk to him. As they met, Azel greeted Dovid with a kiss and a wish for a blessing on him. Dovid told Azel, "I came by earlier, but your wife said you were out." "I am sorry I missed you," Azel said to his friend. Why are you up at this late hour?" Dovid told Azel that he could not sleep. He tossed and turned and could not find rest. "My friend, why are you so troubled?" Dovid began to explain the events of the day and what had occurred.

Azel listened carefully as Dovid went on about the traditions and the laws. All the while, Azel did not say anything. He just kept his head down and listened intently. When Dovid had finished, he looked at his friend, and with one last breath asked Azel, "So how do I mend this?"

After a long pause, Azel answered his friend, Dovid. "Have you ever wondered why we have all this division amongst our people at this time? Have you ever noticed that all the fighting has not been about the truth?" Dovid looked puzzled and did not really know where Azel was going with all this. Dovid inquired of Azel, "What does this have to do with what I have told you?" "Why, it has everything to do with your problems. Why are you so angry?" Dovid, still not completely understanding what his friend was telling him responded, "Because we are losing our traditions and this is the glue that holds our people together." Azel told Dovid, "That is not what I am talking about, and I do not think that this is what is really frustrating you. You fear the truth and letting go to embrace the real issue."

Dovid told his friend, "You are not making any sense. What is this you are talking about? Truth—the truth is in the laws. Is that not what Moses brought down by God from the mountain?" "Yes, it is. Let me try to explain it a little better. If you look at this from a distance, what is the real issue? What is all the arguing about? Is it about this man or about what He represents? You see, it is about fear—the fear that if He is real, we will have to change. His coming has been foretold for centuries, has it not? Dovid responded, "Yes." Azel continued, "Then why would we be surprised if He did come?" "Azel," Dovid interrupted, "My wise friend, His coming has been foretold, yes, that is true, but He was to be the King, and He was to come to save His people. This man, Jesus, did not come from royalty, if I remember what has been said about Him. He comes from Nazareth and is the son of a carpenter. Why would God send His Messiah from a poor family and, more importantly, from that community? Nothing good has ever come from Nazareth."

Azel, getting upset himself, asked Dovid, "May I continue?" Dovid nodded his head, yes, and his friend continued. "You see, we all want to see things our way. I see Him coming one way, you another, and so on. Yet, we are not even willing to accept the possibility of this being the way because He does not look or act like we expect Him to.

We find all kinds of reasons to say that this man is not the Messiah. Over 250,000 people are here in the city for this Passover, and if you ask each one of them, they would give you a different answer as to how and when He should come. Each would give you a good argument as to why they feel that way, but remember, it is not up to you or me as to when or how He will come. It is up to God. We must leave it in His hands for only He knows the time and date. Dovid, would you agree that we know from His Word that a Messiah will come?" Dovid acknowledged the question. Azel smiled. "Good! That is something we can agree on, yes?"

Azel continued, "Then why are we so closed-minded to the possibility of Jesus of Nazareth being the Messiah? Dovid, do you know without a shadow of a doubt that this man is not the Messiah? Are you so sure that you are willing to separate your family and everything you believe important because you are positive? Would you risk your life on it?" Dovid grew silent as he became engrossed in deep thought. "My friend, I believe that we are finding ourselves in the midst of a torment, not because of this man, but because of what He represents. He represents accountability and responsibility for our sins. Notice that since we have been here, little talk has been heard about the Passover. All the discussion and arguments are over one person's beliefs against another's. Who is right? Are you going to allow your beliefs, founded on the laws and traditions, to come between you and your family? Will your convictions and stubbornness become all you have if you lose everything else? Dovid, I am not saying that you are wrong, but I am saying that you may also not be right." Dovid looked at his friend and in a soft voice he whispered, "This is all we have. We must follow the laws. "This is all we know, Azel." "Dovid, we cannot rule out conclusively the possibility that is not the Messiah." Dovid returned a sharp response, "Well, I can."

Azel, saddened by his friend's remarks, tells him, "Then may God help you because our greatest sins are yet to come." Dovid thanked Azel for the time, and said, "I must be getting back now." As Dovid prepared to leave, Azel asked, "Would you still be my friend if I believed as Levi does?" Dovid did not even look back, he just kept on walking. Suddenly he turned back and shouted, "I do not know!" Azel then responded, "Then what this man has spoken will come true." Dovid stopped, turned, and walked toward Azel, and again listened to what his friend was saying. Azel continued, "Jesus told us that brother will be against brother and friend against friend, and the whole world will be at war over our different beliefs. I tell you my friend that I do not want to lose you or any of my brothers. Dovid, are you so set in your ways that you leave no room for the possibility? Tell me, are you more afraid of losing your traditions or your family?" Dovid turned back toward his tent without saying a word. Azel shouted out, "God be with you my friend!" Dovid, talking to himself repeats, "I know the law is more important." Sadly, even though their families spent this Passover together, the friendship between Dovid and Azel ended due to their division of beliefs.

DAY TEN

✝

The change in the climate was evident with the chill in the morning air and the heavy layer of dew from the previous evening. As the sun rose in the east, the dew began to drip off the tents, making little puddles which outlined each tent. It was Thursday morning. The anticipation of the Passover meal was being discussed by all. The women were making preparations for the day of the unleavened bread, and the men were preparing the Passover lamb that would be sacrificed. As the preparations were underway, talk still persisted about Jesus, for whom it was now rumored that the scribes and Pharisees were seeking to have arrested for claiming to be God. The talk again focused on how and when the event would happen. A lot of questions were being asked among the people about Jesus; who He was, what He had said, and the deeds He had done. The reason for this was that the Pharisees were trying to put together a case against Him. Many of the men believed it should already have happened, yet others still thought it would not happen at all.

Dovid, very proud of his lamb was preparing it for the journey into the Temple. People were looking at his animal and staring at its beauty. It was to be shared between four families for the Passover meal this year including Azel and his family, along with two other families who made the trip from their hometown. As Dovid worked on getting the lamb ready, he could not help but overhear the talk about the Pharisees' plot to arrest Jesus. He mumbled to himself, "They should have done this long ago. If they had, maybe I would not have to be going through this upheaval right now with my family." Levi came out to help, and as he did, Dovid looked at his son and told him to put on another layer of clothing. "You are shaking, and your teeth are chattering." Levi returned, and as they cleaned the lamb, he heard the others talking and tried to keep to himself, but he told his father, "You know, when I was in town with mother yesterday, I overheard a conversation with the Pharisees talking about having Him arrested or even killed." Dovid looked at Levi, and with his eyes told him, "We are not going to discuss this." Levi understood his father well and moved on to another topic, but Levi continued to think about how he might warn Jesus about what was being plotted against Him. Working on preparing the lamb for sacrifice was helping to keep Levi and his father from discussing the other issues of the day. They were to leave around mid-day to ensure that the sacrifice would be completed within enough time to get an early start on supper.

Levi and his father headed to the Temple for the sacrifice of the lamb. Dovid, in an attempt to give Levi a sense that their relationship, although strained, was still repairable, asked him, "Levi, do you remember the importance of this day in our tradition?" Levi responded, "Yes, it is the start of the barley harvest and signifies the greatest miracle Yahweh performed out of grace for His chosen. It is our heritage and history. It is also the source of hope for our people, then and now, that someday our Father in Heaven will send the Messiah to free us once more." Levi then looked at his father, and Dovid waited and hoped he would not say that that day had come. Instead, Levi stopped short of saying anything about Jesus. Dovid gave him a smile of encouragement.

As they reached the Temple gate, they were in line for what seemed like hours waiting to enter the court area to have their lamb sacrificed. As the gates opened to allow the next group of people into the Temple, including Levi and Dovid, Levi was overwhelmed by the sights and the sounds. As they entered, Levi noticed a full contingent of Priests throughout the entire Temple. He noticed that even though it was about 1:30 in the afternoon, the Priest's were on the top of the Temple, each in his own corner awaiting the time to sound the horns commencing the next round of sacrifices.

As the gates closed behind them, they all waited to hear the horn of the Priest sound. Dovid told Levi, "This year you can slay the lamb. You are a man now. This tradition will now fall to you." Levi was proud of his father's affirmation of him. Dovid told Levi to hold the lamb just a little tighter, and the anticipation of this great moment had Levi's hands sweating. His heart beat faster and felt like it was coming out of his chest. As the ram's horn blew, the slaughters began! Levi took notice of how the other men did the skinning, how they took out the kidneys, and how the fat was burned on the altar. Levi, almost at the altar, noticed the Priests standing in two rows, one with gold bowls and the other with silver. As the owner shed the blood of his animal, it was drained into the bowls, and the blood was tossed against the base of the altar.

As he moved up in line to take the knife from his father, his hands were shaking. He felt weak and almost could not do it. Dovid gave him a word of encouragement and placed his own hand over Levi's and helped him make the first cut. The blood of the animal was now on Levi's clothes, his sandals, and his hands. As they finished, the animal was placed back in its skin, and Dovid told Levi to place the lamb back on his shoulders. "Let us go celebrate your first Passover as a man,"

Dovid said. As they headed back to the tent, Levi, carrying the lamb on his shoulders, noticed the throngs of people that were still waiting to enter the Temple court. He was looking at the people with a great sense of pride, and they were smiling back at him, because they realized this was a proud moment for him and his family. Levi was also caught up in the different smells as they moved through the area. At times it was overwhelming and even made him dizzy. As they left the Temple, he could not help but notice the stench from burning the fat and the animal's organs.

As they walked back to the tent area, Levi noticed how the smell had changed from the stench of the burnt offerings to the aroma of roasted lamb. He was overcome with a feeling of goodness and a sense that all is okay with the world. He thought just moments ago, "I was afraid and unsure of what to expect, and now I have a feeling of satisfaction and understanding. As evening came, the women had everything set. The food was ready, the families were eager, and all that was left was to enjoy the feast.

As they prepared to eat the meal, it was customary that they eat with their garments tucked under their belts, their sandals on their feet, and their staffs in their hand. They were required to eat in a hurry at the Lord's Passover. Dovid pronounced a blessing over the first cup of wine, and they passed the basin of water around with a towel to wash their hands. It was important that they did this in a reclining position. Customarily, they would gather at a table which was prepared ahead of time, but this time, they moved to a different area in the tent where the food was laid out. After everyone had taken their portion, the plates were removed, and the second cup of wine was poured. Now it was time for a child to ask four questions. In this case, the chosen son was Levi. "Father, why is this night different from all other nights? Father, on all other nights we eat any kind of herbs, but on this night, why do we eat only bitter herbs? Father, on all other nights we eat meat roasted or boiled, but on this night, why do we only eat roasted meat? Father, on all other nights, we dip the herbs only once, but on this night, why do we dip them twice?" Then it was Dovid's turn to give the history of their people and their deliverance from Egypt.

Continuing the ritual, the dishes were placed in front of them, and the second cup of wine was drunk, after which they washed again. They also had two unleavened cakes which were broken and dipped in the charoseth. At last, the lamb was brought out as the main part of the meal, and then the third cup of wine was presented and drunk in accordance with the ritual observance. Once the supper was over, it was customary to sing traditional hymns. Finally, the last cup of wine was poured. It was a special cup that was prepared for Elijah. The meal was wonderful! Everyone commented on how good a job Batel and Eidel did in preparing the Passover meal. Azel and his wife also complimented Levi, saying that they could tell he had done a good job of skinning the lamb and how tasty the meat was.

As the meal ended, very little food was left. As was customary and as prescribed in the Scriptures, any leftovers were required to be burned before the sun rose. When the families said their good nights, Levi was still too excited from the day and could not possibly sleep. He asked his father if he might stay outside awhile. A group of young people were talking, and Levi joined them. As they discussed the events of the Passover meal, the conversation turned toward Jesus. One of the young men told the group, "I noticed Jesus came into the upper city today with His disciples and entered a man's house. What do you think they were doing there?" "I guess celebrating the Passover." Levi asked, "Do you know where they went afterwards?" "No, I did not linger." All the excitement of the day had temporarily distracted him from thinking about Jesus and what would happen to Him.

As they continued to discuss the possibilities, Levi heard from an individual who was running toward the tent area. The young man told them that a group of Temple soldiers were searching for Jesus to arrest Him. Levi jumped up, and in an excited voice said, "What did you say? Who was going to arrest Him? When? Have they taken Him yet?" The young man, caught off-guard by Levi's outburst, took a step back and looked at Levi strangely. Levi realized that he startled the young man. Trying to keep his emotions in check, he spoke more calmly, "I am sorry. Have they already captured Jesus?" The young man told the group, "No, not that I know of; they were heading toward the Mount of Olives when I saw them. I did notice something strange though." "What was that?" "Well, one of His own people was with the guards." Levi told the group, "I need to go." Someone asked, "Where are you going?" "I am going to see if I can find Jesus." "Why?" "To warn Him!" One of the young men shouted, "Are you kidding me?" If the guards know that is your intent, they will arrest you also." Levi did not respond, but just started running toward the Mount.

As Levi hurried toward the Mount of Olives, in the far distance he saw what appeared to be a small light. As he continued to run in that direction, he quickly noticed that the light was not one, but many. Levi began to run faster, thinking that he had to get to Jesus as quickly as possible to warn Him. Levi then suddenly realized that the lights were headed toward him. As he approached the lights, he noticed that it was a sizeable group in guard formation. Levi stopped and stepped aside and waited as the group drew near in the dark. He realized that this was the Temple Guard and they were heading toward the city. He bent over, trying to catch his breath, hoping that he was not too late to warn Jesus. Perhaps they didn't find him. As they passed by, he noticed that someone was surrounded by the guard. Looking closer he noticed that the man in custody was Jesus. His hands were tied, and He was being pulled by a rope. His sandals were slipping and His feet were bleeding. They were pulling Jesus like they were dragging an animal to slaughter. As Levi stood there, he could not move. This event was reminiscent of the lamb they had brought to the Temple just a few short hours ago where people were taking their clean unblemished animals to be sacrificed. He was frozen! No words would come out of his mouth. He was thinking, "I need to do something, I need to say something." He was so shocked by what he was seeing, he could not do anything. As Jesus passed by, He turned His head and looked directly at Levi. It was like seeing something in slow motion. Levi noticed that His eyes were all dark and fixed; no brilliance, no passion like before. As the group passed by, they seemed to be in a hurry. In the distance, behind the group, came two men. When they got to Levi, he recognized them as two of Jesus' disciples whom he had met a few days earlier.

They stopped and asked Levi, "Are you okay?" As they shook him, Levi then broke out of his paralysis and said, "Yes, I am okay. I was coming to warn Him. I am too late." The two men told Levi, "It is okay. It is not your fault. The Lord actually predicted this would happen. He told me Himself. We need to keep on going." As they turned to leave, they invited Levi to go with them. Levi was still in shock, thinking, "If only I had been there sooner, they would not have captured Him. I knew this was going to happen days ago, and I did nothing."

Dovid woke up, feeling cold, and realized that Levi was not in bed. It occurred to him that he did not hear Levi come back in before he fell asleep. He got up and went outside to find him; however, Levi was not there either. Frantically he wondered, "Where could you have gone Levi? What could you be doing at this time of night?"

As he looked around, he saw a group coming toward him, and thought that maybe Levi was with them. Walking toward them in the dark, he noticed that the lights were bright and the group was large. As they moved toward him, they did not slow down and he quickly realized it was the Temple Guard. Stepping aside, he allowed them to pass. He saw Jesus in the middle, shackled as a prisoner. Dovid was surprised by the number of guards they had to transport Him. Even though Dovid did not think Jesus was who He claimed to be, he knew He was not a criminal. So why did they have so many men guarding Him? As they headed toward the gate of the Temple, Dovid thought to himself, "Why are they going all the way down toward the pools of Siloam? Why would they go in from the Fountain Gate? They could have entered at any of the other gates. Having arrested Him, why did they not take Him to the Tower of Antonia? This makes no sense." As he watched them head toward the pool area, he heard footsteps. Someone was now running up behind him. Quickly turning around, and somewhat frightened by the sound of the footsteps, Dovid could now see that it was his son, Levi. Before Levi could tell him what had happened, his father questioned him. "Where have you been Levi?" He told his father that he went to warn Jesus that they were coming to arrest Him. Dovid, with a look of surprise and shock on his face said, "What! Do you realize they could have arrested you?" "Well, no, I did not think about that." "Well, they have already arrested Jesus. They just took Him by here." Levi shook his head, "Yes, I know. I was too late getting there." As they talked, two other men came up behind them. Levi turned and introduced the two men to his father.

"Father, these two men have been with Jesus. They are part of the twelve who are with Him all the time." The men greeted Dovid, and one said, "My name is Peter," and the other said, "I am John." Dovid did not have much to say, actually making it quite uncomfortable for Levi. The disciples distracted by their own concerns, told him, "We must leave and find where the Temple Guards have taken our Lord." Dovid acknowledged them and they left.

Levi turned and began to walk with Peter and John. As he did, his father shouted, "Where are you going?" Levi turned around and told him, "I am also following Jesus." Dovid said to Levi, "Come back here!" Levi turned toward the two men who told him, "You should obey your father. It would be dangerous for you to be seen with us." So Levi returned to his father. Dovid said to Levi, "You are forbidden to follow that man. I have told you this before. Why do you continue to disobey me?" "Father, I need to do this. I am sorry you do not understand, but this is something I must do." Dovid shouted at him, "NO! You will come with me immediately." Levi, caught off guard, looked at his father whom he did not want to disobey, but realized he needed to see this through.

Levi said to his father, "I love you, and I am sorry that I am a disappointment to you now, but I must go." Levi turned to walk away, and Dovid told him once more, "I am not finished. Come back here." Levi returned, and Dovid warned him that his actions would have very serious consequences. "Father, I am a man now. I am thirteen, and I need to make some of my own decisions. You have told me that at this age you were on your own; I am not saying that is what I want, but this is something I must see through."

Levi then turned and ran toward the city. Dovid shouted at his son, "Levi, come back here! I am your father! You will obey me! Levi, do you hear me? Come back!" Once they reached the Temple area, John and Peter told Levi, "You must stay here. It is very dangerous, and we do not want anything to happen to you." Levi objected and pleaded with them to allow him to go with them. Peter chastised Levi, telling him, "Look, we do not want to be responsible if anything happens to you. You need to go back to your father. You must obey his wishes. We cannot let you in with us. It is not safe, and we do not even know what is going to happen to us." Levi agreed with them and left them just outside the Temple entrance. He watched them go in and turned to leave. He got about one hundred meters away from the entrance and turned around, thinking, "Maybe I can get in, and if I am not with the disciples, they will not be responsible if anything happens to me." He then ran back to the entrance.

As Levi reached the Temple, he saw a group of people outside the entrance and asked them if they knew where they had taken Jesus? They looked at him strangely and replied, "No, we do not." A little further down, a man was walking alone and Levi asked him, "Have you seen the Temple Guards and the man they arrested?" He answered, "Yes, I did." "Where did they take Him?" "I do not know, but they went towards the Pools of Siloam." Levi thanked the man, and he headed that way. As he entered the gate, he noticed that people were stirring around, and he asked, "Have you seen the man named Jesus whom they have arrested?" They appeared afraid to answer Levi. "Please, if you know, please tell me." They told him that Jesus was taken to the Upper City to Annas' house. Levi thanked the men and ran toward the Upper City. He climbed up the Hasmonean staircase and reached the house of Annas. He waited outside. He could hear people inside, and many of the guards were standing outside. One of them asked Levi, "What is your business here?" Levi feared the question, and told them that he just wanted to see what was happening. "Go your way and leave this area; you have no business here." Levi walked away, and just then, they opened the door and came out with Jesus. There was a crowd now beginning to develop. As a woman came up next to Levi, she began to shout at the guards to leave Him alone. She screamed, "He has done nothing! Why are you persecuting Him?" Levi looked at this woman and asked her, "Do you know why they have done this?" The woman looked back at Levi and told him, "Yes, they are trying to put Him to death." Levi gasped and tears filled his eyes like pools of water. "Why would they do that? How do you know this is the case?" "I have a friend whose husband is one of the Sanhedrin, and they are getting together all seventy of them, even as we speak, to organize a trial."

As they took Jesus from the house of Annas and headed toward Caiaphas' house, a man shouted out to Annas as he came out, "What you are doing here is a violation of our laws. As a Jew, this man has the right to protection from self-incrimination. Why do you question Him?" Annas responded to the crowd, "I have not violated any law. I did not question Him." With that, Annas went back in his house. The people shouted at him, "You are a liar! You are a wicked man!" Others shouted to the guards, "Where are you taking Him?" They did not answer. The town was now stirring with the speculation of what was happening.

Levi, along with the entire group, followed them to Caiaphas' house and watched as they entered the residence where the entire Sanhedrin was waiting. In the distance, Levi recognized the disciple, John, who was speaking to one of the guards. Both he and Peter gained entrance to the home. Peter remained in the courtyard while John went inside. Levi feared for their lives. He and the others just stood there motionless and more importantly, helpless. They were very cold; it was very early in the morning and the temperature was dropping quickly. Suddenly, the wind began picking up, making it chillier. Levi and the others waited outside, for what seemed like hours, until the sun began to rise.

Levi sought out a man, whose name was Joel, who appeared to know what was happening. He asked him why they were still in the house. Joel explained to Levi that although the Sanhedrin could convict someone, they were unable to put anyone to death. They realized that they must send Jesus to Pontius Pilate. However, because of the law, they could not make the final decision until after the sun rose. Thus, before they could convict Him, Caiaphas, the

Chief Priest, had to wait until the shofar (the ram's horn) was blown, signifying that the sun had risen. As the sun rose and the horn was blown, the Chief Priest came out and announced that they had tried the man named Jesus and found Him guilty of blasphemy. He further announced that they would be sending Jesus to Pontius Pilate for sentencing. By now, the crowd was rather large and enraged, and some were shouting, "Kill Him! Put Him to death!" Others were saying, "Release Jesus! He is innocent!"

As the men came out of the house, Levi, who was in the middle of the crowd, overheard one of the men inquiring of a guard whom he knew, "What just happened?" He told the man that Jesus was asked if He was God, and He said, "I Am." The guard continued, "The Sanhedrin voted and found Him guilty. We are now taking Jesus back to Pilate for sentencing." Levi watched as they brought Jesus out. He was now a little closer, and as they walked by, Levi hoped that Jesus would glance his way, but He did not look at Levi this time. Levi noticed that His face was bright red on one side, with an impression of a hand, where He had been struck. Levi was overcome with nausea as the group walked Jesus towards Pilate's council chamber. Levi saw that the group holding Jesus was much closer now, in tighter formation. They needed to make sure that no one could get to Jesus and try to take Him away.

As the group headed out, Levi saw another one of Jesus' followers, but he was not with John or Peter. He was with the group carrying Him away. But why? Levi could not help but notice that he appeared to be worried. His eyes darted around looking into the crowd, and then he kept looking back at Jesus.

By now, many people were awake and in the Temple area and had heard about what had transpired during the night. They, like many, were interested in what was going to happen. The crowd was electric, and wild looks prevailed in everyone's eyes. As they waited for Pilate to render a verdict, people were betting with thumbs-up or down whether or not Pilate would agree with the Sanhedrin, or release Jesus. As he waited, Levi had time to reflect on the events of the evening, and for the first time in awhile, he remembered how he had left things with his father. More importantly, it was almost midmorning, and he began thinking what would happen when he returned to the tent. Levi thought long and hard about his father's reaction. "How will my father react? What will I say, and how can I tell him and my mother all that has happened?" Pilate came out and told the crowd, "I find no fault with this man," which made Levi and many others very happy, but the Sanhedrin and the Pharisees kept shouting, "He is a blasphemer! He is guilty! We want Him killed!" Pilate decided to send Jesus to King Herod.

As Levi stood and listened to the crowd, a hand touched his shoulder. As he turned to see who was there; he was taken aback and stunned. He could not believe his eyes—how could this be? "I have been worried about you. We did not know where you went. Your family and I have been looking for you all night." "Oh, Azel, I am sorry I have worried all of you, but I have been following Jesus all night. I was present last night when they arrested Him." "Yes, I know I heard. Your father told me this morning." "Did he send you to bring me back? Because if he did... " "No, Levi he did not." "Oh, well okay then, but I tried to tell him last night how I felt, and he would not listen." "Levi, you will have to explain yourself to your father when you get back. I just wanted to make sure you were okay. Tell me what has happened. Why did they arrest Him?" Levi told Azel, "I do not know. Rumors have persisted for days that the Sanhedrin and Pharisees wanted to get Him away from the people because He was creating problems. I heard from some of His disciples that the reason they wanted to arrest Him was because Jesus represented a threat to their power and they felt one man should die for all the people. Since then, they have been inquiring about His whereabouts. They told many people that if they have any information about Him to let the Chief Priest know."

"Levi, you simply must go back to the tent area and let your mother know you are alright." "I will go once I know what they are going to do with Him. I cannot leave now." Azel and Levi then followed the group to King Herod's fortress where the King himself questioned Jesus. Again the crowds were shouting to leave Him alone. Others continued crying out, "If He is God, then He should kill His accusers and walk away. Let Him save Himself. Rabbi, show us a sign that you are really God." Levi was watching the whole thing unfold in front of his own eyes, and could not do anything to help Him. He watched as the Roman soldiers held Jesus and King Herod questioned Him. They placed a red robe on Him, and the soldiers began to slap Him and shout mocking comments at Him. Levi placed his hands over his eyes as they slapped Jesus, cursed at Him, and then finally spat on Him. The crowd was laughing and shouting at Jesus as they repeatedly hit Him, crying out, "Scourge Him," again and again.

After the Chief Priest and the Pharisees spoke to King Herod, they were sent on their way. Levi could not believe it. King Herod would have nothing to do with Jesus! They were sending him back to Pilate. Azel told Levi, "I really expected Herod to have Jesus beheaded like he did with John the Baptist." Levi looked at Azel and said, "Who is John the Baptist?"

Azel told Levi, "I am not completely sure, but some say he was the Messiah. Others say he was Elijah coming to warn the people and prepare the way of the Lord. Some even say he was Jesus' cousin." Levi, now putting the puzzle together said, "Well then, why have I not heard of him before?" "I do not know, but he was killed by King Herod at the request of his wife's maiden." "Well, what did John the Baptist do?"

Levi questioned. Azel responded, "He baptized people in the Jordan River, telling them to repent for the Kingdom of God is at hand. It has been said that John told all those who were at the shore that he was baptizing people with water, but that One would come and baptize them with the Holy Spirit. Many believe that this was fulfilled in the man named Jesus." Levi shook his head, "Yes, that would make sense." Levi recalled that Malachi, the prophet, referred to one that would come to pave the way for the Lord. He recalled the verse that said *"Behold, I will send you Elijah the prophet before the coming of the great and dreadful day of the Lord. And He will turn the hearts of the fathers to the children, and the hearts of the children to their fathers. Lest I come and strike the earth with a curse. "* Levi, still thinking about the importance of the baptism, asked Azel, "What is the significance of being baptized?" Azel responded, "I really do not know. All I know is that this is something that His disciples and many of the followers are doing." As they continued to walk, Levi again questioned Azel, "Did you do it?" "No, I have not." "Do you know anyone who has?" "Yes, many of my friends, and even Jesus was baptized as well. John baptized Jesus in the Jordan some time ago."

Jesus was brought back to Pilate and the crowd was now cursing and spitting at Him, calling Him names and laughing. Pilate, after questioning Jesus again, brought Him out and told the crowd, *"I find nothing wrong with this man."* Levi and many of His followers shouted with joy and yelled, "Let Him go then!" But the Chief Priest and the Pharisees claimed that He was a sinner and not a friend of Caesar's. They continued to shout to Pilate that he must put Him to death. Pilate asked them again what crime this man had committed. The Pharisees shouted that His crime was against Caesar and the Roman Empire.

As Pilate took Jesus back again, the crowd was shouting at each other once again. As the outcry from the crowd grew even louder, they began to push and call each other names. Levi just stood there. He noticed that the Chief Priest and the other Pharisees were attempting to rile the crowd. Levi watched as the Chief Priest turned to look at the crowd, then looked in Levi's direction and smiled. Looking at the group of Holy men, Levi noticed that a familiar face was trying to get the attention of the Chief Priest. It was the same disciple Levi saw with the Pharisees, Levi asked a question out loud. "Does anyone know who that man is?" "Yes," one of the men said, "He is Judas, one of the twelve." The Chief Priest would not even talk to him and many of the other Priests just pushed him away. Levi noticed that Judas had thrown a purse at the Chief Priest; as it hit the ground, all the coins scattered. This created a panic among the people who were now dropping on the ground, frantically trying to pick up the money. As they did, Pilate came out with Jesus. Looking at Jesus, it was obvious that He had been beaten.

The crowd grew silent as the realization fell over them that Jesus had been beaten beyond recognition. They could not believe what they saw. Levi was now in complete shock as he stood with tears streaming down his face. He glanced at Azel who was white as a sheet. Levi noticed a look of desperation as Azel looked over at Levi. Their eyes locked, but neither said a word. The air, which had been warmed by the bright sun, had now become unmistakably chilly as the sky turned to gray. Jesus was standing still; His hands were tied and blood was dripping down His face from His head which had been adorned with a crown of thorns. Levi and the crowd were devastated. Even those, whom just moments ago were shouting to have Him put to death, were now straining just to get a look at Him. Many of the women who followed Jesus were crying out loud, pleading for God to stop this madness. Levi could not believe what they had done to Him. It was as if this was not the same man they had seen just a short time ago. The Roman soldiers had severely beaten Him and scourged Him beyond recognition. The silence was deafening. The crowd was waiting for what would come next.

From behind, Levi heard someone call his name, causing him to jump. He turned to see his father and burst into tears. He could not believe that in addition to everything that had happened today, the fact that his father would come looking for him was somewhat overwhelming. As he faced his father, gripping him with both arms, he turned away from Jesus. Burying his face in his father's coat, he wept so much that he could not gain control of himself. As a young man, he had never seen anything like this before. His father tried to tell him, "It is going to be okay," but Levi would not let go. "Levi, please release me. You are holding me so tight I cannot breathe." Levi calmed himself as he heard Pilate begin to speak.

Pilate announced to the crowd, "I have punished this man and still find no fault with Him." He continued, then speaking to the Chief Priest, the Pharisees, and the people, he said, *"You have brought this man to me, as one who misleads the people. And indeed, having examined Him in your presence, I have found no fault in this man concerning those things of which you accuse Him; no, neither did Herod, for I sent Jesus back to him; and indeed nothing deserving of death has been done by Him. I therefore chastised Him and will now release Him."* At this, Levi turned once again to his father; the tears would not stop flowing. Because of his emotions he could not even look at Jesus. He turned to see Azel now, also in tears, as many of the people were. Because of what Pilate had just said, they all felt a sense of relief. The crowd now began to cheer! However, the Chief Priest and the Pharisees shouted at Pilate, *"Away with this man, and release to us Barabbas!"* Azel looked at his friend, Dovid, and inquired, "Who is this they want released?" Dovid replied, "I do not know who they are talking about." Azel asked the man standing next to him who was also shouting for Barabbas' release, "Who is this they are wanting released?" "He is a rebel who tried to set up a rebellion against the Romans and has been accused of murder." Azel looked at Dovid and Levi and whispered to them, "Brother, I cannot believe they would want him released." Now the crowd, who once had been asking for the release of Jesus just a few moments ago, was chanting, "Release Barabbas! We want Barabbas released!" As they continued to shout, the hair on Levi's arms stood up causing a chill which caused goose bumps all over him. He knew that this was not good. Dovid looked at Azel and rolled his eyes at him in an attempt to tell him, "We should go." Azel did not know how to respond.

Pilate asked the crowd, *"What should I do with your King?"* The reply resounded, *"Crucify Him; crucify Him!"* Then he said to them a third time, *"Why, what evil has He done? I have found no reason for death in Him. I will chastise Him and let Him go."* But the crowd continued, insisting and demanding with loud voices, that Jesus be crucified.

Pilate handed down the sentence that it should be as they requested. After releasing Barabbas to them, Pilate then had Jesus taken away to be crucified. At the precise moment the sentence came down, the sky went dark and a haze came upon the entire land. Pilate looked up and realized that things were changing. He then looked at the crowd, quickly washed his hands, and left the platform.

As the crowd broke up and each went their own way, the Pharisees and other members of the Sanhedrin mingled together. The consensus was that they felt they won a big battle. Their arrogance and the smug look on their faces was unmistakable. They laughed and hugged each other, and stood around accepting congratulations on their success. Levi, now beside himself along with the other believers, just stood in shock and stunned silence. Levi asked Azel and his father, "Do they know what they are doing? They cannot possibly know who this man is." His father looked at his son and told him, "Son, this man was nothing more than a man, and although He was a good and kind man who helped people, He is going to be put to death for His teachings. It is a good lesson; leave the preaching and wisdom to those who know it best. That is one of the reasons that I wanted you to become a Pharisee, so that someday you can make decisions like this."

"Father, you do not know what you are talking about. He is not just a man—He *is* the Messiah. I know this because I not only know the Scriptures, but I also have seen the people He has helped, and I have listened to Him speak to the crowds. He speaks with authority as if He wrote each and every word Himself. He speaks better than any Pharisee or Chief Priest I have ever heard. You should get on your knees and plead for wisdom to know the truth. You, of all people, should know that when God spoke to you on the journey, this is what He was revealing to you. You have listened, but you—like most of the people here today—are not willing to see the truth."

Dovid looked at his son with a sense of bewilderment as if to say, "Who are you to talk to me that way?" Levi, realizing what he had done, and not wanting his father to have a chance to chastise him, continued, "I know this is not what you want to hear from your son, but I feel very strongly that I need to let you know who this man is and what He represents." Dovid's puzzled look and his anger grew rapidly. Azel looked at Dovid and did not respond at first. Dovid's hands were trembling uncontrollably, and he was ready to explode as he told Levi, "You and I have a very different way of looking at life, Levi. You do not know anything. You are wrong, and you have abandoned everything I have worked so hard to give you." Just then Azel jumped in and told Dovid, "Remember, my dear friend what I said the other day— tradition or family?" Dovid looked at Azel as if he was looking right through him and said, "I can see I am too late.

You both have lost your minds. I wish you both good luck. We will be leaving to return home in the next few days." He looked at Levi with tears streaming down his face and announced, "Your mother will be disappointed you did not come to say goodbye to her." Levi, now firmly planted in his beliefs, told his father, "Tell Mother I will come back later today and talk to her." "No! You are no longer welcome in our family Levi! You have made your decision about what you believe, and with whom you are placing your alliance. You have chosen to follow a man who will be dead by the end of the day!"

Levi then responded to his father as a last effort to help him understand, "While I walked with the disciples, Peter told me many things about Jesus the Christ." He told his father that the disciples had left everything to follow Jesus and that Jesus had told them that, "*Whosoever leaves houses or brothers or sisters or father or mother or wife or children or lands, for My sake and the gospel's, who shall not receive a hundredfold now in this time.*" Levi stated that John had also told him this, "*With man nothing is possible, but with God everything is possible.*"

Dovid turned and walked away. Levi, not wanting to cry in front of his father, turned the other way and asked Azel, "What will we do now?" Azel placed his arm around Levi and told him, "Do not worry. We will work this out with your father." Levi told Azel, "I am not so sure after the way I just spoke to him. I do not know if he will ever speak to me again."

Levi and Azel saw the disciple, John, and went over to him. He was with two women who were both weeping. Levi greeted John and introduced Azel. In turn, John introduced the two women as Mary Magdalene and Mary, the Mother of our Lord. Levi greeted both of them and dropped to the feet of Mary and said to her, "I am so sorry about your son." She continued crying, but told him, "My son, please stand up. It will be okay."

Mary told Levi, "Do not worry; the Lord must suffer many things. For this reason He came into the world so that we may have eternity in Heaven." Levi was now looking at Mary and the other woman when a man came running up to John and whispered something in his ear. John, looking very sad, thanked the man and he left. Mary asked John what was wrong. He told her that Judas was dead. When she asked what happened, John told her that he had hung himself.

Levi did not understand, for too much uncertainty and chaos surrounded them this day. Mary simply closed her eyes in pain. Suddenly, they brought out Jesus, along with the two other prisoners. They were taking Him to Golgotha where they would crucify Him. The crowd was still rather small as Jesus passed by carrying His own cross. He had a garrison of guards surrounding Him to prevent anyone from getting close to Him. Much of the crowd was supportive of Jesus, but they barely uttered a word. Many of the women mourned His scars, and the men just watched casually as He passed. Levi could not believe that just a few days ago he had seen Jesus smiling as He passed Levi and his mother on the way back from the Temple. Now Jesus was beaten and scared almost beyond recognition. His mother, Mary, was so sorrowful that she almost fainted. John grabbed her just before she fell to the ground. Jesus, looking at her, could barely stand. Levi did not comprehend the extent of His wounds. As they passed, His back was so badly beaten that Levi could actually see bones protruding, and blood coursing so quickly that it reminded him of the bloodshed he had seen just the day before during the sacrifice of the Passover lamb. The road, spotted with Jesus' blood, was now lined with people who had received word of His imminent crucifixion.

The crowd, which was calling for His release just a few hours ago, was now taunting Jesus. They threw barbs at

Him, "If you are the Christ, save yourself." Levi could not believe what was happening. The crowd was spitting and laughing at Him. These were some of the same people who were following Him during His walk. They were proclaiming Him *King* just a few days ago; now they are calling Jesus an imposter or a fake. Levi asked Azel, "Why are these people doing this? I do not understand." Azel told Levi, "People are like lost sheep that follow where the main group leads them. If they stand up for what they believe, they may be outcast, so it becomes easier to follow the crowd than to stand alone."

"Azel, aren't these some of the same people who were healed by Him?" While they were shouting, Jesus toppled to the ground. He was so weak that He could no longer stand. One of the guards asked a man to help carry his cross. Levi shouted, "I will do it," but the crowd was so loud that no one heard him — no one that is, except Jesus, who looked directly at him. Even in the midst of the pain from his injuries, and the blood dripping into his eyes from his head wounds, he noticed Levi's attempt at kindness, but he did not say anything. Levi, now overcome with sorrow, stopped. People were pushing by him. Levi was trying to follow the crowd, but they pushed him causing him to fall to the ground. Levi was pulled up by Azel who asked him, "Are you alright?" Levi looked at Azel and told him, "I cannot do this. I refuse to go any further. I cannot watch them crucify Him." Azel said to him, "I understand. We will stay here then." Levi told him to go on ahead. "It will be okay. I need to go back to the tent now. Our Lord is going to His death." Azel told Levi, "No, I will stay with you," but Levi insisted he go. Levi then turned and headed back towards the valley area where his family would be.

In the distance, as he walked, he heard screaming. He stopped and knew it must be Jesus. He was grieving so much that he fell on the ground and pounded the dirt and screamed himself, "God, why are you doing this? Why would you send this Messiah to us to have Him killed? You told me that your glory would be fulfilled in this city, but you are allowing your Son to be put to death. I do not understand this. Why God? Why?" As he lay there, he felt a presence around him and then opened his eyes to see a shadow behind him. He turned to look up and saw his mother. "Levi, my son, are you alright?" He jumped up and grabbed her and fell completely apart. "Mother, I do not know why they are killing Him." His sobbing and gut-wrenching emotions were raw, as a feeling of brokenness swept over him. Levi told her, "I do not know what to believe and what to do anymore."

Batel comforted her son, "Levi, it will be okay. God has a plan, and we must accept that. He will find a way to lead His people, even if it means that we do not understand." Levi arose, and Batel wiped away his tears. A feeling of great love swept over her and she said, "Levi, I came to find you because I felt in my spirit that I must come to you and bring you home for you were in great distress. God has seen fit to have us here during this time and this season, and He will let us know when He is ready to show us His plan." "I am glad you came for me, Mother. I was feeling very much alone. What about Father, does he know you are here?" "No, I did not see him. I just left and came to find you." "Where is Eidel?" "I left her with our neighbor." As they returned to the tent, Levi went inside and laid down, exhausted. He fell asleep, but was awakened just a few hours later by what seemed like an earthquake and someone crying loudly. He arose and came outside into the darkness. He went to his mother and asked, "What time is it?" Thinking he had been asleep for a long time, she told him that it was about 3:00 in the afternoon. Levi then told her that the sky was so dark that he thought it was much later. "Someone was crying so loudly that it awakened me. I could feel the ground shaking. Who was crying? Was it Eidel?" "No, it was not your sister, but the wind blew like I have never heard it before, then the rain came down for a few minutes, and then it stopped. I have never heard the wind howl like that before." Levi looked at her and said, "Maybe it is God who is angry with the world for what they have done. Mother, do you think they have crucified Him yet?" "Yes Levi, I am sure that they have. My only hope is that they bury Him before the sun goes down." Levi was once again reminded of what had happened and what he had seen.

He asked his mother, "What is it that you believe about Jesus? Do you think that He was the Messiah, or do you agree with Father that Jesus was a fake?" Batel looked at Levi and paused for a moment before responding, "Levi, I will tell you this..." From behind her, she heard, "What is it you will tell him?" She turned around and saw Dovid towering over her. "I was going to tell him what I believe." "Good, because I am also interested in what you have to say. More importantly why is this boy here? I forbade him from returning to our family." Batel, now angry, shouts at her husband, "I brought him home! He is our son!"

Batel's face paled as she calmed down. She looked at Levi and said, "I am not one hundred percent convinced that this man was the Messiah, but I do know this, on our walk that day, He spoke things to me that no one else knew. I also know that you are a bright young man and that you know the Scriptures well, and I believe that you would not do something that would go against the law or your father unless you believed in your heart that it was true. I also know that so many people have been saying that this man has done great miracles including raising people from the dead. This could not have happened unless it was from God."

Dovid now looked at his wife and said, "I cannot believe that even you, my wife, would go against me. All these years I have been the head of this household, and you have obeyed my direction. Now you are letting your son and these people change your mind about who God is and what we, as a people, believe and follow. How could you go against me and the traditions of our people?" "Dovid, I am not going against you. I do not know for sure what is true at this point, but I do know that people have seen this man raise the dead, and I know no ordinary man could do that. Dovid, do you really feel no possibility exists for this man to be the Messiah?"

"I am telling you that this man, were He the Messiah, would not have been crucified. God would not have allowed Him to be beaten and treated the way He was. If Jesus were the Christ, He would have come from Heaven on His horse with His crown and His army to free us. Instead, we have a man who has been spit on, beaten by the Romans, and put to death. That cannot be our Messiah." Dovid continued, "Enough of this foolish talk. Night is almost here, and we need to complete our evening meal and prepare ourselves to go to the Temple tomorrow for the counting of the Omer, our first fruits. What is done is done! We will entertain no more talk about this man whom the Pharisees have proven is just a man, not God."

DAY ELEVEN

✝

A s the day broke, and the bright red sun rose in the east, it cast shadows against the homes and buildings, but the most picturesque shadow was on the Temple itself. The chaos turned to tranquility, and all was quiet again in the city. The events of the prior day still hung heavy in the air. As was the custom, Dovid prepared to bring his first fruits to the Temple for the second day of the unleavened bread. Eidel asked her father, "Why do we do this?" He replied, "It is the forty-nine-day period in which our forefathers were awaiting to hear from God after their liberation from Egypt. On the fiftieth day, they would receive the Torah." Eidel then asked, "Father, why is Levi not helping with this?" Dovid explained, "Levi has decided that he no longer believes in the God of our forefathers. He has chosen to follow a different way and can no longer participate in the traditions or feasts." Hearing this, Levi was upset, but would not speak. Instead he left the area and went toward the Mount of Olives hoping to see the disciples and ask them more questions. He was still upset about what he had seen yesterday, and was still trying to make sense of his newfound beliefs.

Levi looked back on Jerusalem and felt empty. He recalled that just a week ago, he had been so excited about traveling to the city for the Passover with all that it meant for him and his family. Now, he not only had his ideals changed of what he believed, but he had been estranged from his father. The city appeared to be dark and cold, no longer a place of comfort and peace, rather one of turmoil and confusion. Levi said aloud, "I was excited about the opportunities ahead of me. I was glad my family had made it through the difficult journey and that we were all together. Now I am by myself. Everything I have believed in, everything I thought I knew from Scripture has changed. My family has been divided by what has happened here this week in the Holy City. I thought that coming here would bring our family closer to you, our God—not further away. How can this one man, who was sent to unite His people, divide them so easily?" Levi thought, "Life will never be the same again. What Jesus spoke about the city and the times, has already started to come true." As Levi sat, picking up small stones and throwing them against the ground, he surmised, "My life will never be the same again."

Levi questioned, "What if I am wrong like my father has indicated? What if this man died, and He is not the Christ? What if I have given up everything for what I believe, and I am wrong?" Fear began to overtake his sense of what he believed. "Could everyone in the city, who saw these things and listened to Jesus, be deceived? Perhaps, but how will I know that all the signs listed in Scripture have been fulfilled?" Levi thought back on what the Scriptures have stated about the Messiah's coming. "Our people have been waiting for five hundred years for the Lord to send us His helper." He thought back to the prophet Isaiah and what he wrote about and how it applied to this generation, "*How beautiful upon the mountains are the feet of Him who brings Good News, who proclaims peace, who brings glad tidings of good things, who proclaims salvation, who says to Zion, your God reigns! Your watchmen shall lift up their voices, with their voices they shall sing together, for they shall see eye-to-eye. When the Lord brings back Zion, break forth into joy, sing together, you waste place of Jerusalem! For the Lord has comforted His people, He has redeemed Jerusalem. The Lord has made bare His holy arm in the eyes of all the nations; and all the ends of the earth shall see the salvation of our God.*" Levi thought that Isaiah was correct, "Jerusalem is a waste place now in his eyes, but now what? If God truly has sent His redeemer, and they have killed Him, what will become of Jerusalem and what will become of me?"

Levi prayed, "LORD, I am fearful of what will become of me and what will become of our people. LORD, please offer me a sign to remind me that what I have seen and heard is true and that your loving kindness will be shown upon your servant and all your people. LORD, forgive me for my disobedience toward my father, for I wish not to break the law you have set before me, but to uphold it. I ask that you cleanse me with hyssop and make me white as snow in your presence, for you are the Almighty God, the Father." Levi then recited the words of King David from the Psalms: "*To you Lord I lift up my soul, O my God, I trust in you; Let me not be ashamed; Let not my enemies triumph over me. Indeed, let no one who waits on You be ashamed: Let those be ashamed who deal treacherously without cause. Show me your ways, O Lord; Teach me your paths. Lead me in your truth and teach me, for you are the God of my salvation; On you I wait all the day.*"

As Levi finished praying and thinking about all he had seen and heard, he was still confused about the truth. Had he made a mistake or was he, and what seemed like a few others, correct? One thing is for sure, he needed to speak to the others who were with Jesus and by going to Bethany, he hoped to find them and obtain answers.

As he got up and headed to the town of Bethany, he went to the house of Lazarus, the friend of Jesus—the one Jesus raised from the dead. Surely he would have some insight into what this was all about. Then he thought of Jesus' disciples. "They must be close also. Maybe I can talk to John again and find out more about what they saw and what Jesus did. I need to find out answers so that I can be sure of what I believe." Levi had become fearful that everything he had done was now in vain. Now that Jesus was dead, what was the truth, and who were they to follow?

Levi saw a woman walking toward the house and introduced himself. She told Levi that she was Martha, the sister of Lazarus. He told her that he had been outside her home when Jesus was there, before heading into Jerusalem. He told Martha that he had been following Jesus ever since. "Have you seen His disciples?" She replied, "No, I have not." As he continued to talk to her, he felt comfortable in telling her about his feelings. He could see that she was upset, and he asked her what he could do to help. She looked at him and said, "Child, your kindness is greatly appreciated, but there is nothing you can do. Our Lord is gone." As they walked toward her home, she continued weeping and saying, "He saved my brother, but did not save Himself. I do not understand why He did this. Jesus has saved the world, but not Himself. Now, what are we to do?"

Levi asked Martha, "What do you mean He saved the world, but not Himself?" "My child, do you not know what He did here? Not too far from this home on the hill, the Lord raised my brother from his death. My Lord came to my home after my brother had been dead for four days and raised him." Levi looked at her and said, "I have heard this all over town. Can you tell me what happened?" Martha told him, "Jesus came and when He got here, I ran out to meet Him and told Him that His friend, my brother, had died. Previously, He had visited with us for many days and we had come to know the Lord well. He had told us many things about the Kingdom of God, and we believed that He was the Messiah. Knowing this, when my brother was sick, we had sent for Jesus. At first, He did not come. Then, I was told that He and the disciples were coming to see my sister Mary and me. I ran out to meet Him and told the Lord, 'our brother and your friend Lazarus is dead.' I also knew that, even though my brother was dead, whatever He asked of God would be given to him." Levi, listening intently, stopped her and asked, "Well, what did He say?" Now, even through her pain and sorrow, she had a glistening in her eye as she told him, "He looked at me, and said, '*I am the resurrection and the life. He who believes in me, though he may die, he shall live. And whoever lives and believes in me shall never die.*'" Stunned, Levi looked at Martha with his mouth open. Martha continued, "Then Jesus asked me the question that we all have to ask ourselves, the question that you are asking today without saying it aloud. He asked me, '*Do you believe this?*'"

Levi inquired, "What did you say to this?" "I said what I believed; yes! The Lord then requested, '*Show me where they have laid Him.*' He instructed me to get Mary and meet Him there. Mary ran ahead, and when she saw the Lord, she fell at His feet crying. He was so deeply moved by our sorrow that He also cried. When the Lord saw that our hearts were broken, He then commanded that the stone be rolled away. He called on the Father to thank Him for hearing Him and praised Him for allowing Him to show the people that He was sent by Him. He then called my brother out of the tomb, and my brother was alive again!" Levi asked, "Where is your brother? I would like to meet him." "I do not know where he is now. He had to leave. The Lord told him to go away for a while as the High Priest was seeking to arrest him and kill him. He was a threat to their way of life, as was the Lord." Levi could not believe it; his head was now filled with wonder and more questions.

Martha said, "Child, you came here in hopes of hearing about what had happened to us. You have heard the truth. I have told you what the Lord did; now the question you have to ask yourself is, 'Do YOU believe this?' You were not here personally to see the miracle, but you have heard it from many people, so why do you question what you know in your heart to be true?" Levi spoke honestly, "It just seems hard to believe that anyone can raise the dead." Martha agreed, "Yes, that is true of a normal man, but the Lord was sent by His Father, so with God all things are possible."

At hearing this, Levi realized that he had heard this before from the disciples. Martha affirmed him, "Your questions are certainly normal. If you had been here, would you feel better because you would have seen it for yourself?" Levi nodded in agreement. Martha continued, "In your own mind and heart you already have a sense that this is true, do you not?" Again, Levi nodded, "yes." "Then, why are you not listening to your heart?" "I do not know," Levi replied. "You are right, but my father and others whom I have known, tell me Jesus is not the Messiah. Why would they say that if He is? I guess what I am saying is, why do I see it and they do not? That is my question; why can I see the truth and they cannot?"

Levi, after saying this, recalled the words of Isaiah and told Martha, "Perhaps this is why He opened my eyes to see His glory. *'Lord, who has believed our report: and to whom has the arm of the Lord been revealed? He has blinded their eyes and hardened their hearts, lest they should see with their eyes, lest they should understand with their hearts and turn, so that I should heal them.'* Martha looked at Levi and remarked, "It appears you are listening to your heart and searching out the truth. Go in peace and be careful where you go and to whom you speak."

Levi questioned Martha one last time, "May I ask you one final question?" Martha agreed. "If all this is true, and you know that you will see Him again on the last day, then why are you so sad?" "Child, all my hope was in His words and deeds. When I was with Him it seemed like time stood still, and whatever worries I had disappeared. I loved to sit at His feet and listen to Him, to hear Him laugh at stories, and then to hear the Lord speak of the Kingdom and what heaven was going to be like. I loved sitting and just looking into His eyes and seeing them dance with excitement as He talked about the Father. He told me things about myself that I never even knew. How do I go on now? What do I have to anticipate now?" Levi responded, "You have eternity to listen to Him when you see Him again." Martha smiled and told him, "You are going to be a great witness for the Lord." Levi smiled and thanked Martha again for her time and wished her well.

As Levi headed back toward town, his head was filled with information about what the Lord had done and more about what He had said. Could Martha have been the answer to his prayers just a few hours ago? He thought over his own feelings, and now, he felt rejuvenated by her testimony. Upon his return, he had to try to convince his family that they were mistaken about Jesus. Levi thought, "He is the Lord in the flesh, or was the Lord. But what will I say? What will I do to convince them? Some way must exist to accomplish this. I do not want to be alone, and I do not want to be separated from God either."

As Levi arrived at the Mount of Olives, it was almost dusk and the skyline behind the city was bluish-green and hazy, much like Levi's mind at this point. He was physically tired, as well as mentally drained, so he decided to sit a while. He leaned against one of the trees and reflected about the day with all the confusion about the truth and who knows it and who does not. He contemplated how he would change the minds of his family and others he would meet. He must be strong. He also realized that, with all his training, this must be what the Lord would have him do. Levi was thinking, "It is all about trust. What I believe is right, not just because of what I have seen and been told by others, but because I have faith in His word and promises. This truly is what God must have meant when He told us about His power and glory in the city."

Now, as he sat and continued to look over the city, he reflected on what King David must have seen when he stood there so many years ago? He began to recite, "*I sought the Lord and He heard me, and delivered me from all my fears.*" Suddenly, he felt all his fears and doubts were gone. He continued, "*Oh, taste and see that the Lord is good; blessed is the man who trusts in Him!*" As he repeated this over and over, he leaned his head back, closed his eyes, and fell asleep.

Levi got a chill and awoke to the cold in the darkness, suddenly unaware of his surroundings. He could not see anything. He sat up, and now with blurred vision, began to focus on the lights in the distance and realized it was the Holy City. As Levi arose and tried to warm himself, he began to think, "How long have I been here?" Levi realized that he must get back to the tent area. He knew his parents would be worried. Then he paused and realized that he had been separated from his family by his beliefs. Levi, for the first time in his life, felt empty and had nothing to look forward to when he returned home. He was actually saddened by the prospect of going back. He stood around for a few minutes and looked at the city in the dark, from the top of the hill. The torches and lanterns burned against the cloud cover of the sky, making the city glow with a haze rarely seen. It no longer appeared cold and dreary. In fact, as Levi looked at the Temple, it resembled the outline of a king's crown created from the bright glow of the lanterns as they shined up in the clouds and reflected back down on the white marble. In that spectacular moment, Levi felt that God's promise to reveal His glory and power in the city had come to fruition. Even though Levi was certain that God had fulfilled His promise from so long ago by sending the Messiah now to free his people, he wondered, "Why are the people not watching for the Messiah as God had said? Why did they not listen to Jesus when He spoke?"

As Levi reached the tent area, he could see that his family was asleep and he did not want to wake them. He stayed outside by the fire, which was almost out, and stared into it, seeking a word of encouragement to help him deal with his overwhelming loneliness. He prayed silently to himself, asking for help, "Father, you have shown me so much, and I believe that you have sent your Son. Please, Lord, help me deal with my anger and pain. Help me feel whole again. Lord, I know that I am no one, but please grant me this wish that I will be able to reconcile with my parents and help them see your Son, Jesus, for who He is. Lord, I want to do your will. Help me as you did so many others, to have the right words to say to help my parents and others see your goodness through your Son, Jesus."

Levi then closed his eyes and was hoping to hear something as he did before, some kind of sign, rain—anything to let him know his prayer had been heard. There was no sign, no flickering in the light of the fire, nothing. Levi opened his eyes and nothing; he thought, "Has God not turned His ear to my prayer? Does God wish me to wander around without the benefit of my family? What will it take for God to hear me?" In the meantime, Levi realized that he would have to make it on his own. He laid back down and fell asleep once again.

DAY TWELVE

✝

L evi awakened to the sound of people getting ready for the day. The sun was not up yet, but some people were packing and getting ready to return home. Others just wanted to get into town to make their purchases for the week for their return trip home. As the sun rose and the sky cleared, Levi was reminded of the days when they first began their trip to the Holy City.

His mother came over, and in a quiet voice, asked, "Where were you last night?" He told her of his trip to Bethany and his encounter with Martha. Then Levi asked her, "What happened here last night?" She said, "Nothing really. Your sister was concerned about what had happened to you, but we told her you were with friends." Levi asked his mother, "Have you thought anymore about what we discussed yesterday?" Batel asked, "Why do you continue to talk about this? You are not going to change your father's mind, and I must follow his ways. He is my husband."

"Mother, how do you know when something is true or false?" "I am not sure I understand what you are asking me." Levi pressed, "What do you consider when making a decision about whether to believe something is real or not?" "I guess I ask questions. I listen to what others have heard or seen, and finally I pray about it." "Good! Then what do you believe about this man, Jesus?" Levi's mother replied, "I do not want to do this Levi." "Mother, please; I just want to understand your reasons." "What do I believe about Him? Well, some said He was the Christ, that He performed miracles." "Okay, then you spoke to Him yourself." "Yes, but I did not know it was Him until you told me." "Yes Mother, I know, but Jesus spoke to you about things that others did not know, correct?" "Yes!" "Okay, what about your heart?" She replied, "What about my heart?" "What does your heart say about this man? Is He the Messiah?" "Levi, my heart does not matter. I must follow your father's ways. He is my husband, and the family is what is most important." "So, if Father believed and said Jesus was the Messiah, you would agree, but since he does not believe, you cannot." "Well, it is more complicated than that." "No, it is not Mother! I thought so too, but I was wrong. I listened to my heart, and I spoke to people who were traveling with Him and to others who were healed by Him, and they all say the same thing; He is the Christ. So why do we allow others to make our decisions for us when we know what we believe is true?" "Levi, you just do not understand. I love your father, and I took an oath before God that I would honor him in everything that I do. I will not change that." "Mother, I understand. I really do, but I think the real reason for me was that if I proclaimed it out loud, then there was no going back. People may not agree, but if it is what I believe, then I must be true to that belief." Batel thought about what her son had said and could not argue with him. She did not respond. She just told him, "I need to prepare the morning meal now," and she began to work.

Levi had one more question for his mother, "Please just answer this for yourself; has Jesus fulfilled what was written about Him?" She responded, "Yes, right up until they crucified Him." Levi responded, "God told us that His Glory would be fulfilled in the City, and He accomplished this by revealing His Son to the world." As he continued to speak, his father came out and looked at him and just nodded at his presence. He walked over to greet his wife with a kiss. Levi really felt like he was separated from his family, thinking that even a stranger would receive a better greeting than this. Levi walked over to his father and said, "Would you at least greet me as you would a stranger?" Dovid stared at Levi without saying anything. Levi turned his back to his father.

Dovid questioned Levi, "Tell me Levi, you are a learned man, so where is your Messiah now? Oh yes, He is dead in a tomb. He preached that He was the Son of God. Would God allow His Son to be crucified on a cross? I told you He was not the Messiah. Now the people who followed Him are scattered like the birds in the sky. They will no longer show their faces in the marketplace, for they are ashamed and are wanted by the Pharisees. Your Messiah, who healed the sick and raised the dead, could not do for Himself what He did for the others. He was a fake. You placed your allegiance with a sinner. You should get face down on the ground and ask God for forgiveness, and ask Him to show mercy on you. You should praise God that He did not strike you and the others dead where you stood."

"Father," Levi responded, "My Messiah does live. I have seen Him and so have you, but you are reluctant to acknowledge Him. Why is that?" Dovid glared at his son and said, "I have not seen the Messiah. I have seen a man claiming to be the Messiah, but I have seen no sign of His power." "Then why did you run out of the Temple when He spoke and prophesized to the Pharisees?" "I left because He was speaking blasphemy," Dovid shouted. "Father, may I tell you a story that Jesus, Himself, told to a group of Pharisees and others?" Dovid responded, "Please, by all means, let me hear this great wisdom." By then, Batel and Eidel had come in. They were all sitting on the ground and listening as

Levi continued, "A man sitting at supper with Jesus and the Pharisees commented to the group, *'Blessed is he who shall eat bread in the Kingdom of God.'* Jesus responded to him and the ruler of the Pharisees in whose house He was. *'A certain man gave a great supper and invited many, and sent his servant at supper time to say to those who were invited, 'Come, for all things are now ready.' But they all, with one accord, began to make excuses. The first said to him, 'I have bought a piece of ground, and I must go and see it. I ask you to have me excused.' And another said, 'I have bought five yoke of oxen, and I am going to test them. I ask you to have me excused.' Still another said, 'I have married a wife, and, therefore, I cannot come.' So the servant came and reported these things to his master. Then the master of the house, being angry, said to his servant, 'Go out quickly into the streets and lanes of the city, and bring in here the poor and the maimed and the lame and the blind.' And the servant said, 'Master, it is done as you commanded, and still there is room.' Then the master said to the servant, 'Go out into the highways and hedges, and compel them to come in, that my house may be filled. For I say to you that none of those men who were invited shall taste my supper.'"* Levi looked at his parents and said, "This story is referring to all those who reject Jesus as the Son of God. You see, He came so that all would know that God has answered our prayers. Yet, we are too busy to do what He asks and to follow His commands. Why? Because we are so involved with our own worldly things that we do not want to part with them." Levi stopped and looked again at his parents who were now quiet. Batel asked, "Where did you hear this story?" To which Levi responded, "From Peter, one of His disciples. But to be honest, I did not know what I was going to say to you, and these words just came to me. I will tell you that if we are not careful, we will be left with our worldly things, and God will not invite us to the supper."

Dovid said to Levi, "This is the most insulting thing I have ever heard. You are telling me that God sent His Son into the world, and those who were well-versed in God's work and His commandments, spoke to this man almost daily, witnessed the things He did, and yet they rejected Him as the Messiah? This was all because they were more concerned with their own materialism?" "Yes, Father. That is what Jesus said." With a thundering voice, Dovid responded, "If these are the men of God, why do they not recognize the Messiah who God has sent?" "I just told you; they are more concerned with their power and possessions and do not recognize Him, but not because the signs are not there! They are, but they do not see them because their hearts are hardened by their greed and power. That is what the story Jesus told is about." Dovid said, "Levi, yes I understand what He is saying, but again, if Jesus was the Messiah, why did God allow Him to die?"

Levi asked his father, "Did He not heal the blind, the sick, and the lame, and finally raise the dead?" Dovid responded, "That is what people are saying." "Father, one of your best friends attested to the fact that He had done these things." "Okay, so what does that make Him—God?" "Why did God let our people wander in the wilderness for forty years? Because they were stiff-necked and stubborn. Father, please believe me; I know what I am telling you. The things Jesus has said and done are a testimony to His Majesty. I beg you to open your heart and mind and see the things He has done for what they are. God told you that He would do great things in the city. I believe this is what He was talking about." "Levi, how can this be?"

"Father, Jesus spoke of many things, and toward the end of His life, spoke that the Temple would be destroyed and rebuilt in three days." Dovid gave his son a strange look. "What? Who can do that? It took many years; how can this be?" "Father, according to His disciples, He was speaking

of Himself as the Temple of God, the resurrection of life."
"Levi, stop right there. That is enough! I will not tolerate this
any longer. You are speaking foolishness." Levi requested
to share one final thing with his father. Dovid stood up and
said, "No, I will not listen; I have heard enough."

Levi shouted, "Jesus foretold that the Temple veil that
divides the holy of holies would be torn in two!" Dovid
walked away, but Batel asked, "What are you talking about
Levi?" "Jesus predicted that the Temple veil would be torn
in two from top to bottom right down the middle, and it
happened the day of His Crucifixion." His mother asked, "So
what does that prove?" "It proves that the things He spoke of
are true; that we will no longer have to have the Chief Priest
go before God on our behalf. We now have access to God
through the Messiah." Dovid told Levi, "You must leave
immediately, and do not come back. You are possessed."
"Father, please." Dovid commanded, "I said leave!"

Levi walked away dejected and hurt. He was crying now
and could not even believe this was happening. People were
looking at him like he had leprosy. As he walked away, a
crowd of people who were standing around, and had heard
the conversation between Levi and his father, were parting
like the Red Sea as he moved through them.

As he picked up his head, he could see all those people
around him, and not one of them showed him any compassion. He cried out, "What are you looking at?" As he turned
around and looked back towards his tent, his mother was
crying and appeared helpless to rescue her son. The crowd
now shouted at him, "You are one of them, one of His
followers. You believed His false teachings and His satanic
deeds. Where is your Messiah now? What will you do now?
Go be gone before you bring a curse on this place."

Levi said nothing. He just walked amongst the crowd
until he reached the end of the tent area and headed toward
the Temple. The final shouts were faint and almost out of

range. He heard, "Maybe we should stone him!" Then he thought, "Lord, why are you doing this to me? Why do you punish your servant? I know that you have a purpose here. Please give me wisdom in this matter. I beg you Lord; do not leave me out here all alone, with nowhere to go. I prayed that a sign would be given to me. I have followed your ways all my life. Please God, help me." Levi fell on the ground in the hot sun with no other soul in sight and cried. He was so upset and alone that he cried to God in anger, "Why are you doing this? You are making me a fool. Have you not heard my plea? Have you left me for dead? What have I done to you God that you would leave me in my time of trouble? I have stood up and spoken the truth and alienated my entire family and all my friends. Was I wrong? Did I not speak the truth? Was I wrong about Jesus? Is He not the Messiah? Were the Pharisees and the scribes and all the people right? Did I fall into Satan's trap?" Levi then screamed and cried as he looked up to God, "Father, why do you not love me? Please tell me why you do not care? I am here Lord. I have been here. What do I do? Please help me Father. Please do not leave me here all by myself. I am so scared. I do not know where to go or what to do. Please! Please!" Levi laid limp, face down in the dirt, exhausted and emotionally drained. He could not move, but somehow the rhythm of the wind and the warmth of the sun had given him a feeling of peace. He could not explain it, but somehow he felt better. Maybe he was just so tired that he had no more emotion or energy to give. It was mid-day and no one was walking by. He was completely alone, and it was deathly quiet—so much so, that Levi felt a calming in his spirit. Suddenly, he was able to focus on what he needed to do. A voice within him told him that he should go into the Temple area and pray. As he arose, he brushed off the dust from his clothes, wiped the tears from his eyes, and headed towards the Temple.

He reached the southeastern side of the city and entered by the Fountain Gate. Climbing the staircase of Hasmonean to the Upper City, he recalled the last time he had seen Jesus and the events of that day. He passed by the home of Caiaphas when he saw two of the women whom he had seen before with Jesus. They were running the opposite direction shouting, "He lives! He lives!" The women created quite a stir. As the people were trying to determine what they were yelling about, they disappeared into the crowd.

Levi entered the prayer area. Once inside, he dropped to the ground and began to pray. He closed his eyes, and once again thanked God for all the blessings in his life. He began to express to God in his own words his thankfulness for His greatness and His power, and was thankful for all that He had bestowed upon him. He now reflected on the events of the week and what he had seen and heard. As he prayed, he told the Lord, "I am so blessed to be here in this place at this time. You have shown me so many great things that it overwhelms me. Lord, thank you for giving me the under-standing to deal with all that I have seen. I am in awe of you and how much you love us all. I am a weak man, and I have not done your will as you have requested; however, I know that you have sent your Son into this world for those of us who have gone astray. Lord, I humble myself before you and request that I may be as your servant Isaiah when he said, '*Lord send me.*' I will do whatever you want. I am grateful for the opportunity to serve you." Thank you for answering my prayer and placing me with all those who have seen your glory and believed it." As Levi spoke these words, he felt restored in his faith. He no longer felt weak and scared. Clearly, Levi felt something rising up within him, and he felt like a new man.

As Levi was finishing his prayers, he heard people shouting in the distance, "He is risen! He is risen!" As he remained silent, the sounds grew louder and louder. Clearly, a crowd was stirring. Levi asked God to intervene on his behalf with his father and help him find peace with his family. As he concluded, he opened his eyes and turned to the right to look behind him and saw a man praying next to him. The man also finished and turned to the left. They locked eyes—it was his father, Dovid. Levi shouted, "Father!" Dovid, in tears, clearly had been on his knees for some time because he was experiencing difficulty in standing. Levi leaned over and helped his father to his feet. Dovid was moved by his son's compassion. Levi asked him, "Are you alright?" Dovid nodded, "Yes." As he was about to have a conversation with his father, two men were coming through the Temple shouting, "He is risen!" The people were asking who they were talking about. They yelled, "Jesus, of course!" Levi looked at his father with anticipation. Dovid, who was holding on to Levi's garment, let go and started walking away. Levi was torn. Should he go after his father, or follow the men in the street? He decided to go after his father.

Levi ran yelling, "Stop! Please Father, stop! I need to tell you something." Dovid stopped and turned. Levi told him, "I am sorry that you are angry with me. You have told me that you are very proud of me for understanding the Scriptures, and that you believed I had the wisdom of a Pharisee. Dovid said, "Yes, what of it?" "Well, if that is true, why do you feel that I am wrong about this?" "Levi, you have a lot to learn. You are my son, but I do not have to agree with you, and in this case, you are wrong and you refuse to accept the fact that this man was a fake." "Father, these men are saying that Jesus has risen. He foretold that this would happen. He was a prophet, was He not?" Dovid looked at Levi and said, "We have been over this again and again. Just drop it. You have disappointed me, and everything that our family was looking forward to is now lost. My ability to lead my family is gone, and I have lost my son." "Father, what must I do to convince you that what I am telling you is true?" "Levi, nothing you can do will convince me of that." What if Jesus *has* risen? Then would you believe it?" "I need to go." Levi asked again, "Would you then believe it? Please, Father. Do not walk away. I have more to say." Dovid continued to walk away. "I will show you that He is who He claims to be." Dovid just walked away shaking his head in disbelief and thought to himself, "How can this be? I have asked you for a sign and a blessing to bring my family back. I get nothing but more lies and deceit, and my son and I are growing further apart. Why are you doing this to me? I have done your will. I asked that you turn your ear to me and hear me, Lord. Answer my prayer. I want my son back, and I want to stop all this nonsense." As Dovid walked away, Levi frustrated, began to look for the men who were claiming that Jesus had risen.

As Levi caught up to the men, they were in the street telling everybody that, even though Jesus had been crucified, He was alive again. They were being questioned by everyone, "How can this be? Where is He now so we may see Him?" "We did not see Him ourselves. We were told by the women that were at His tomb that He was not there, and that two angels told them that He was alive." The crowd was really growing hostile. "What? You are crazy! Let us go see for ourselves." "We have been there, the two men told the crowd the tomb is empty." The crowd then headed outside the Temple towards the place where Jesus was laid to rest. When they arrived, they saw some people looking around, and many others praying in front of the opening. Most were lying face down, praising God for this miracle. Levi could not believe it. He still was not sure what had happened, but he knew the body was gone.

Levi and the other people who were present, were trying to figure out what had happened. Levi just listened as many asked their questions. One man shouted, "How could this be? Raised from the dead? It appears that someone has stolen the body." "Yes, the crowd yells," but one of the men shouted back, "That could not happen. An entire Roman Guard was surrounding the tomb." Some of the Roman soldiers were still there trying to take control of the chaos, but as they were questioned, they said the followers came while they were asleep and took Jesus' body. The crowd yelled, "Those thieves! They should be stoned." Others asked, "How can that be? Was the whole Guard asleep at the same time?" The believers shouted back, "You know what happened here! Why not tell the truth? He has been raised from the dead!"

Levi now began to see what God's glory had foretold. He had raised His Son from the dead, but Levi did not have all the pieces of the puzzle in place yet. In fact, no one did. The Roman soldiers were being criticized by the crowd. Fearful of a riot and for their own safety, they left the tomb unsecured. After they left, many curious people were looking inside and saw the clothes laid on the bench, neatly folded with no sign of His body.

The Pharisees who thought that the frenzy would die down once they had Jesus killed, now had a new problem. Everyone was talking about Jesus, and it was worse than before. Levi was listening to the people from both sides. They were now more vehement than ever. As Levi stepped back and focused on what was being said, he realized that he was not the only one who had been separated from his family. The people in the entire city were separated by this man who was hung on the cross. Levi had to find the disciples and sort things out. If all this was true, they would know where Jesus was and what had happened.

As the crowd moved away and back towards their homes, Levi saw a man who was telling everyone earlier that Jesus had risen. Levi greeted him and said, "How did this happen?" The man told him, "I do not know. I was just told to go into the Temple and the upper city, and let everyone know that He has risen." "Do you know any of the disciples?" "Yes, I know Andrew." "Do you happen to know where they are?" "Why do you ask?" "I need to speak with them. I have been following the Lord for some time now, and I hope to get some answers about what has happened." "I do not know if I should say, and I am not really sure." Levi interrupts, "Please! I must go to them. They are the only ones who can help me." The man told Levi, "I heard that Jesus told the woman to have the disciples meet Him in Galilee. I do not know where exactly, but I hope that helps. This is all I know." Levi thanked the man and started to run off, as the man shouted, "Blessings and God be with you."

Levi, now heading towards Galilee, realized that it was almost one hundred miles from the Holy City. He could not do this alone. He would have to wait until the disciples returned. Disappointed, he headed back to the tent area where his family would be. As he approached, many of the people who were cursing him and calling for his stoning just hours ago, were now shouting for joy and claiming that they knew all along that Jesus was the Messiah. Levi thought it was interesting how the crowds were like lost sheep, following the masses anyway they went, including going off a cliff. As they are celebrating and cheering, Levi notices Azel. He came to greet him. Azel asked Levi, "What do you make of all of this? Can you believe it? He has risen." Levi somberly told Azel, "We have been given an amazing gift to be here in this time and see the Glory of God, and we are responsible now to do what He shall have us do. I tell you this Azel, I feel that our time here and now is about to change, that everything we have known will be different from this moment on. We will no longer be accountable to the Pharisees, Sadducees, or even the High Priest since we now have Jesus Christ of Nazareth."

Azel responded, "Praise God for His Glory." Levi inquired, "Azel, have you seen my father?" "Yes, I did some time ago. I believe he went back to the market area."

"Why?" Levi asked. "No reason, I guess. I think he needed some time alone." Levi said, "Then I will go to my mother and sister and spend some time with them. Thank you for being so understanding and for your friendship. It means the world to me." Azel replied, "Levi, you are always welcome in our home, and if you ever need a place to stay or someone to talk to, you know where I will be." Then Azel told Levi, "Please be safe; we will be leaving in the morning to head back home." Levi responded, "I understand, and I will. God willing, I will see you there shortly." Azel warned Levi, "Do not allow your family to be separated by this event. Work hard at making sure your family understands what happened here. I pray that they will see God's mercy and greatness and come to know His will. I told your father that his traditions should not get in the way of what is true and what is real. I only pray that he, and all those who were here this week, come to realize it. If we are not careful, those who witnessed God's Glory here, and do not accept it for what it is, will be separated from Him forever." Levi shook his head and told Azel to have a safe journey, and prayed for Azel and his family. He hugged Azel and patted him on the back, and then headed towards his family's tent.

Levi came up behind his mother and placed his arms around her. She did not need to see who it was, she knew instinctively. She shouted, "Levi, you are back!" Turning around, she asked him if he was alright and if he was hungry. He said, "Yes, I have not eaten anything since this morning, and I am famished." She gave him some food, and they talked about what had occurred. She asked him, "Do you really think that Jesus is alive?" "Yes, I do. In fact, when I speak to His followers, I will have more information to give you and Father. Where is Father?" "Well, Levi, he is trying to make sense of all that has happened. I told him that I would not allow this family to be split apart, and that he needed to at least find out why so many people believe in this man. Then, once and for all, he can decide what is true." Levi shook his head and asked, "So, do you now believe?"

"I do not! Anyway, what I find interesting is that both you and your father want me to side with each of you. I can tell you this, when it comes to taking sides, I will always be on your father's side. I have told you this before. When I have tough decisions to make, I will always rely on your father's judgment to help me through. Is that clear?" Levi said, "Yes," but he was hoping his mother would see the truth, and help heal the family. Batel could see that Levi was upset about the conversation, but nonetheless, she had to be on her husband's side. Whether or not she believed in what her son had told her, or what she had heard from the others, was irrelevant.

Levi then went out and played with his sister and her friends. For the first time in a long time, he was laughing and having fun playing with children his own age. He had forgotten how much fun it was to be happy. No one there would judge him for what he believed. They just wanted to be friends.

The children were playing games and yelling, and having so much fun that Levi forgot what time it was, and all his worries had temporarily disappeared. Batel now called Levi and Eidel back for supper. When they returned, Dovid was in the tent, and all the laughing had stopped. Levi was back to being serious again.

Dovid greeted Eidel and nodded to Levi. Levi said, "Good evening, Father." Levi still felt very uncomfortable, but he did not say much during supper. Once they finished the evening meal, Dovid told Batel that he was going to spend some time with the other elders. "I will be back before long," and got up to leave. Just a few short weeks ago, Levi would have been invited to go with him. Once Dovid left the tent, Levi began to feel sick to his stomach, but did not want his mother to know. As he got up, Batel asked Levi, "Where are you going?" He replied, "Outside for a walk." Batel called him over and said, "Do not lose heart. I know he loves you, but he still holds close to the traditions of our people and is having a difficult time." Levi understood, but it did not make it any easier for him, because he felt like his father did not love him any longer. Levi put his arms around his mother. She realized that her son was still a young man who needed his parents. Although he possessed a great understanding of the Scriptures, he was still learning about life.

As Dovid returned, he came in and saw the family sitting there, playing and talking. He looked over at Levi and said, "I need to see you outside a minute, Levi." So Levi arose and followed his father outside. Dovid said, "Let us go for a walk; I want to talk to you." As they walked along, initially nothing was said. Then Dovid spoke, "Levi, I know that things between us have not been so good, and it hurts me that we cannot seem to make it right. I know you have your beliefs about Jesus, who many, including you, believe is the Christ. I have tried to see what you see, but I cannot. I do not know if it is my upbringing or my own stupidity that keeps me from seeing what the rest of you see, but I just do not see it. I have been pretty hard on you, and I know that has made it difficult for us to talk. Son, I love you with all my heart, and I would like nothing more than to mend our relationship, but, we have been separated by our beliefs. You see, I believe in the God of Abraham, Isaac, and Jacob. You believe that this man, Jesus, is God. That is a fundamental difference in what you and I were taught in the Temple. How can I say, and how can you say, that everything we were taught—the traditions of our forefathers are wiped away by this man? You see son, I cannot see this man taking God's place in my heart. I only know one God." Levi listened carefully, and for the first time that he could remember, he was not intimidated by his father and did not feel that he was being criticized for what he had come to believe.

"Father, you are correct and I understand what you are saying, but even Isaiah himself said that God told him, '*do not remember the former things, nor consider the things of old. Behold, I will do a new thing.*' Father, God has always promised us a Savior, and we have been waiting for Him all these years. So why when Jesus comes along, who fulfilled many of the Scriptures, do we not believe it is Him? He was sent to bring good news of the Lord, and He has spoken it in the synagogues and the Temple. He has given sight to the blind, allowed the deaf to hear, helped the lame, set the captives free and finally, raised the dead. So, why do we not accept Him for who He is? This is why He came and we want our freedom from the Romans, not from our sins or infirmities. We expect God to do things our way, and if it does not meet our needs, then we reject it." Dovid looked at Levi differently than he had in some time. "Levi, you are a very smart young man. What you say makes sense, and I really wish I could believe in what you say; however, I just have a hard time believing this man is the Christ."

"Father, remember the words of your servant Moses in the Torah who said, '*Trust in the Lord, for He has brought you out with a mighty hand, and redeemed you from the house of bondage, from the hand of Pharaoh, King of Egypt. Therefore, know the Lord your God.*' We must know that God will do the unexpected, not because He is trying to trick us, but because He is faithful and has promised us a Savior. Those who see this man and call Him the Christ, will be blessed forever. He has spoken that if you have seen Him, you have seen the Father."

Dovid told Levi, "You see, this is why I get angry. No human has ever seen God and lived." Levi looked at Dovid and said, "Yes, I know. That is why I believe He is telling the truth. He told the Pharisees that He is the great I AM, and they did not believe Him. Father, it took me some time to realize something." Dovid asked, "What is that?" Levi replied, "I cannot convince you who this man is, and you cannot convince me that Jesus is not who I believe Him to be; yet, we continue to move apart in our attempt to do so. God gave us all free will to accept Him or reject Him. I choose to accept Him today as the man named Jesus of Nazareth. There will always be those who will or will not accept Him, but that is your choice." Dovid shook his head, yes, and then said, "I will listen to you, and I will pray about it, and we will see if things change. Right now, I just want us to be together." Levi placed his arms around his father and looked up to God and mouthed, "Thank you." They headed back to the tent.

Batel was waiting, unsure of what Dovid was going to say to Levi, and most assuredly not knowing how either would react. Earlier, she had prayed, asking for God to heal her family and to help restore peace between her husband and her son. As they returned, she noticed that neither appeared to be angry nor fighting. She was glad to see that they were walking back *together*. As they reached the tent, although not speaking to one another, they were close to each other. As they arrived, Dovid looked at Batel and announced that he was hungry. "Let us take out some dried fruit and bread. Levi and I want to eat." She smiled and said, "I would be happy to do this for my men." They both looked at each other and smiled.

There was no doubt that the two had not settled the conflict between them; however, they had made some concessions on what they both believed. Dovid told Batel, "I think we will be heading back home with the remaining group a day from tomorrow." They should have gone back with Azel, but decided to wait to try to first work things out with Levi. Dovid told Levi, "We must go back with the others, because we do not want to go back alone. Too many people are being attacked. The pilgrims are not safe by themselves, particularly around Samaria." Levi told his father that he had decided to stay in Jerusalem for a few extra days. He wanted to see things through. He had secured a place with a local family who was willing to take him in for awhile. Concerned, Dovid asked, "Levi, what of your studies? What about your dreams of being a Pharisee?"

Levi told his father, "I will continue my education, but I will need a new mentor now. Do not worry; I will conclude this when I return." Again expressing concern, Dovid did not want to reprimand Levi, because he knew that he would only push him further away. They worked out a plan for Levi's safe return, but the rest of the family was forced to go back now, since they could not afford to stay any longer. In addition, many of the pilgrims had already left the Kidron Valley, creating a dangerous situation for the remaining families. Safety only existed in larger numbers.

Dovid told Levi, "Tomorrow, I would like to meet the family you are planning to stay with." Levi agreed that they would meet them in the morning and finalize everything. Batel was not so sure this was a good idea; nonetheless, she went along with what her husband had decided.

As night fell, and Levi drifted off to sleep, his prayer was for God to grant him a clear understanding concerning his future. Was it to be here in Jerusalem or back in Scythopolis? Batel quietly talked to her husband and wanted to know what had happened during the conversation with Levi. Dovid told her, "I still do not agree with him, but I have done as you asked. I will give him some time to realize that he is wrong about this man and come to his senses. Our family will be united once again." Dovid continued, "You know Levi has a strong belief in this man and is convinced that He is the Christ. I can see the conviction in his eyes. He truly believes in what He says. With all his understanding of the Scriptures, it is apparent that he has grown up. I will give him some time to work this out in his mind and return home." Batel kissed her husband and responded, "Thank you for understanding and doing what I have asked. Our son is growing up, and if what you say is true, then it should not be long before he realizes he is wrong and returns home. If, however, he is correct, well then...." Dovid cut her off, "We are not going to go through that again, are we?" Batel said, "No," and told Dovid good night. She snuffed out the lantern and placed her coat over her shoulders and went to sleep.

As Dovid slept, he dreamt that he was flying around and could see over the Temple and could hear people's conversations. He dreamt that the High Priest, Caiaphas, was talking to the Pharisees and the scribes telling them that they had a big problem. "How could the tomb be empty? We put an entire Guard in front of it, and his body is gone. Who took it? What happened to it?" Dovid listened as the scribes told the High Priest that the Roman Guard was present, but the body was removed. The Pharisees asked how this could this be possible. The scribes told them that according to some of the Roman Guards, a great earthquake occurred, and the stone was moved. Then a bright light came out of it, and they all fell on the ground with fear and trembling. It was as if they could not see anything; as if they were blind. In his dream, the Chief Priest then asked them, "Do you believe that this man was raised from the dead, that He is the Messiah?" One of them said, "He spoke often that He would be in the ground for three days and then be raised up." "Nicodemus, are you telling me you believe this to be true?" The man looked around the entire group and paused for a moment and then said, "Yes, yes I do believe He was raised from the dead." As Dovid's dream continued, he was standing in front of the tomb and peered inside. It was so dark that he could not even see his own hands. As he tried to focus his eyes, he heard a voice behind him, "You were present. You saw it! Why do you still not believe?" Dovid turned around and almost jumped out of his skin. He saw Jesus with His bloody face, and holes in His hands, and feet. Dovid looked at Him and became fearful. Jesus continued, "I saw you there while they crucified me. Is that not true?" Dovid closed his eyes and replied, "Yes, I was present, and I saw what they did to you." "Why did you not tell your son these things? Dovid of Scythopolis, open your eyes and look upon me." But in his dream, Dovid could not look at Him because His voice was so piercing. He was so frightened that he placed his hands over his eyes and heard again, "Dovid, open your eyes and see my glory." Dovid awoke in a cold sweat, screaming, "I will not open my eyes! Go away from me!" Batel, now awake, also held her husband and spoke to him, "It is okay. You just had a bad dream." Dovid looked at his wife and said, "Why must I be tormented with this? I just want to be left alone so I can live my life with my family in peace." Dovid attempted, but had a difficult time going back to sleep. Sleep did not come easy this night.

DAY THIRTEEN

✞

B y morning, many of the pilgrims had finished packing their belongings and were saying their final goodbyes to friends and family before they returned home. It was a busy time, and people were scurrying to get on the road. Dovid arose and walked outside to get some fresh air and was in deep thought thinking quietly to himself when Levi came up behind him and said, "Good morning, Father." Dovid literally jumped in the air. "I am sorry Father. I did not mean to startle you." "Sorry Levi, I did not hear you come up." "Is everything alright?" "Yes, son, it is. I was just in deep thought." "I understand completely, Father." Although things were still not back to normal, Levi felt that just the fact that they were talking was a big step. "I had planned to go into the city today to see if I could find the disciples and find out what they have heard or seen."

Dovid, looking distracted and confused, agreed with Levi, "Yes, you should do that. I am going to the Temple also. I think it is a good idea." Levi looked at his father with a confused look of disbelief. "Father, do you want to come with me?" Dovid, now focused on his own thoughts answered, "No, I did not mean that I was going to the Temple. No, I have things to do. You go ahead, but remember, I still want to visit the family you will be staying with and we are leaving tomorrow morning. I want you to spend some time with your sister as well. She is young and does not understand much of what is going on here." "Okay, Father, I will do that." Levi headed out after the morning meal. As Levi walked away, Dovid called to him, "Levi, I have a question." "Yes, Father, what is it?" "How did you know that Jesus is the Messiah? I mean, how did you really know without a doubt?" Levi paused for a moment and then responded, "I knew when I read the words of the prophets who had foretold of His coming that the deeds He would do and the things that He had done all fit, but it is more than that. When Jesus speaks He has a way of making you feel like everything is going to be okay. It is the way He interprets the Scriptures. It is like no one I have ever heard. I knew it the first time I heard Him speak and looked into His eyes and felt His love for all those who were present. Finally, not one person could dispute His ability to not only quote Scriptures, but to talk about God, as one who has a personal relationship with Him. That is something I have never heard. Father, let me ask you a question? How do you know that the sun rises each day, even when you do not see it through the clouds?" Dovid thought for a moment, and then said, "I know because I have seen it every day. Even when it is cloudy, I know because I have seen it through the break in the clouds." "Yes, but how did you come to trust that the sun was present all the time?" Dovid replied, "Because I was taught that God created it for us." "Exactly!" Levi shouted. "You trusted that God made it for us, and so it is with His Son. He has made Him for us as the LORD our God has promised He would, and I know because I have trusted in His Word. I have spent time seeing what He says and does. I trust that what I have observed and heard is true. Maybe the best way to explain what I am saying is to say this, 'I know, that I know, that I know Jesus of Nazareth is the one He claims to be.'"

Dovid told Levi, "Thank you for your examples. I have much to think about." "Father, are you still struggling with this decision?" "Levi, I do not know if I will ever understand. I am trying, but I just find it hard to accept that any human could be God. I just do not understand it." Dovid thinks to himself, "Why do I keep being shown this man? Does this mean I could be wrong about the traditions and the laws?" Then Dovid comments out loud, "No, I am wrong; He is not the Messiah. What was I thinking?"

As Levi went into town seeking to find the others, noticeably less people were now present since most of the pilgrims had already returned home. Thus, finding the disciples should have been easier, but many people were still along the roadside trying to sell their goods and services. Some wanted Levi to make a purchase, while others were telling him that the end was near and to repent, because God was going to destroy the world for its wickedness.

Levi recognized a few people who were close to the disciples and asked if they knew where to find them. Most shook their heads, no, while others just walked away, fearful that someone—a Pharisee or scribe, or even worse a Roman soldier—might see and arrest them and have them put to death. The Holy City was a difficult place to be in that moment in time. The chaos and turmoil that had taken place over the past few days had put everyone on edge. The entire city was split by what had happened. Most of the Jews did not believe in Jesus' deity, and would tell you that it was a hoax. They maintained that He was never really dead, and that if He was resurrected, why had He not shown Himself to everyone? Why only to the people who followed Him? Others claimed that they had seen Him, and that He would be returning very soon. Now crowds were gathering at the site of His Crucifixion and at the tomb to fall on the ground and pray. This made it very difficult for the Roman soldiers, as well as the Pharisees, to maintain order in the city.

Levi searched everywhere he knew they might be, but could not find them. He continued to look in the Temple area around the upper city, then the lower city. He even walked up toward the Mount of Olives and headed toward Bethany, but no sign of them existed anywhere. Some told Levi that they believed the disciples had returned home from where they had come, quite possibly to the Sea of Galilee where they had first met Jesus. Levi was really confused. He decided that he would go toward Emmaus where many said they heard that Jesus was seen with two of the disciples.

As Levi prepared to go northwest toward Emmaus, he stopped by the tent area for some supplies and told his parents where he was headed. His father told him, "Why not wait until tomorrow, and we will go with you? We will be heading home. The hour is getting late, and you should be getting your rest, my son." Levi replied, "Father, I would like to make it before dusk this evening, and head back in the morning if they are not there. If they are there, I would stay somewhere close by with them." Batel spoke to her son, "Even if they are there, I am not so sure you should be around them. It has been said that their lives are in danger, and I do not want anything to happen to you. I would feel better if you waited and left with us in the morning." Levi did not want to disappoint his mother, and he was tired, so he decided to stay with the family for the evening.

The evening went well. The family had a traditional supper, followed by the reading of the Scriptures. Levi could not help but wonder how things would change, if any, since the Messiah had come. Would the traditions that his family and the families before them had practiced be different? The one thing that Levi knew without question was, God had sent His Son into the world to bring mankind back into a relationship with the Father. To Levi, that was the thing of importance that was different. He felt that, for the first time, he not only knew God from reading the Torah, but he knew

Him more intimately from listening to Jesus. How would that affect his relationship with his earthly father? What would change? Would they still go to the synagogue, and would they still follow the old family rituals of the Sabbath?

Batel came to Levi and asked him questions about what was being said around the city. "Tell me about how He was resurrected. Did He just get up and walk around? Has anyone seen him?" She was very concerned about how this all took place. Levi told her everything he had heard, and was optimistic about meeting up with the disciples to find out more. His mother was now more than an inquisitive bystander. She was really interested in finding out the facts because, for the first time, she realized that women were playing a big part in Jesus' ministry. She was never allowed to have time in the Scriptures—that was the man's responsibility. Now, all this was changing because of women like Mary, Joanna, and Mary, the mother of Jesus, who were witnesses to His resurrection. Jesus told them to go tell the others. If what she had heard was true, then all women were accepted by Jesus and God. This intrigued Batel, causing her to have a desire to learn more. She was hungry for more information which enriched her knowledge and understanding for the truth. Levi told her, "I do not know much more than that, but I have seen and met His mother, Mary, and also many other women to whom He has spoken, including Martha, the sister of Lazarus whom Jesus the Christ raised from the dead. Martha had studied at His feet before, and He has told her many things about the Kingdom." "Do you really believe that He would accept me if I believed also?"

Levi told his mother that God had sent Jesus as it was foretold, to free mankind from captivity. Maybe the captivity was not just from the Romans; maybe it was from the laws and traditions as well. Jesus had told the people that He came for the poor, and to heal the sick and brokenhearted. Batel listened intently and smiled as Levi told her all he knew about Jesus. Batel noticed that Levi had an excitement in him as he witnessed to her. This excitement reminded her of when he was just a boy, how his face lit up, and his voice had great anticipation in it. She thought to herself, "My, how excited he is about Jesus. I want to know that kind of passion for something also."

Because they had to arise early to head toward home, Eidel and Batel got the beds ready with the blankets and the other garments. Batel told Levi, "Your father has not been sleeping well these last few nights. Something is bothering him. I cannot put my finger on it, but something is wrong." Levi suggested, "Maybe he is struggling with his own thoughts on what has happened here." "Perhaps," Batel said, "but he needs his rest for the long day we have ahead of us tomorrow, and it will be daylight before we know it."

DAY FOURTEEN

✝

In the morning, the family arose, packed everything away, ate some dates, pomegranates, and bread, and then finished packing up the donkeys. Then off they headed toward home. Levi anticipated meeting up with the disciples and hopefully learning more, but that would have to wait until he could locate them. The first order of business was to get to Emmaus and determine if they were in the city. Levi hoped that if they were, they would be willing to spend some time with his family to help them understand who Jesus was, what he had done, and help explain His ministry to his family. After all, they had been with Him three years; they knew Him better than anyone. Levi was determined to lead his family and friends to what he knew was the truth.

Dovid told Levi, "Once we arrive in Emmaus, we will make sure that you find your friends before we head on home." They headed north, but it was difficult because the rugged terrain was not the normal path to which they were accustomed. Dovid warned his family, "We must use caution since we will be traveling by ourselves. We have to stay close, because there are those who would cause us harm."

Once they reached the town, they found out that the disciples were not there, and no one had seen them. Levi was upset. He asked his family if they might stay awhile to find out if anyone else might have seen them. Dovid agreed, as they needed a break from traveling if they were to continue on the road home. "However," Dovid explained, "We cannot stay long because we must meet up with the remaining group. We do not want to go through Samaria without them. That will be the most difficult part of the trip."

Levi agreed, so he hurried around trying to find out where the disciples might be. Levi continued to ask around whether anyone might know of their whereabouts. Most replied, "No." However, he ran into one man named Jacob who said that it had been rumored that Jesus had been there with two of the disciples, but was no longer there. Levi looked dejected and asked the man, "Do you know where they might have gone?" He said, "No, but check at the inn; they might know where they are." Levi headed over to the inn and inquired whether anyone had seen the disciples. The gentleman behind the table told him, "No, I have not," but another man standing by asked, "Whom do you seek?" Levi told him, "I am looking for the men who were with Jesus of Nazareth." "Oh yes, Jesus was with Cleopas. He is one of His followers, along with his wife, Mary, but they left." Levi asked, "Do you know where they went?" "I am not quite sure, but I did hear that they were headed to Bethsaida." Levi knew that town well. The town was located on the Sea of Galilee, and he could easily make it there. It was about twenty miles away, merely a half a day's trip from his hometown of Scythopolis. Levi now realized that he would return home with his family and then travel on to Bethsaida. As he went back to meet up with his family, he was reminded of another story in which Jesus told a crowd, "Knock and it will be opened; seek and you shall find." Levi was not going to stop until both of these had been accomplished.

Levi and his family caught up with the others who were returning home. By the time they arrived back in Scythopolis, they were exhausted, but Levi was anxious to get on the road to Bethsaida. He told his father and mother that he would be leaving the following morning. Dovid, who wanted to go with Levi, realized that he had to stay home because the trip had taken three days longer than they expected, and he needed to get back to work to make money to support his family. However, he was concerned about Levi's safety. He told Batel that he wished he could accompany Levi on this journey to make certain he was safe. Batel did not respond. As evening fell and they were preparing for bed, they all realized how good it was to be home. Even Levi was glad to sleep in his own bed again. He still felt strange though, because so many memories dwelled in this home. He thought about all the time spent studying the Torah with Ishaq and his father. These seemed to be distant memories now. He thought back about his life and realized that everything was different now. God had changed him, his feelings, and his relationship with his family—especially his father. They no longer agreed on religious requirements. Levi had much to learn, but he felt that God would lead him, and oh, if only he could spend time with the disciples and maybe even Jesus! If so, then he would receive all the information he needed to know about the things God had in store for him. Levi yearned to be like Martha and Mary. Like them, he longed to sit at the feet of the Lord and learn from the Master. Just the thought of this possibility was worth everything to Levi.

Preparing to leave the next morning, Levi was saying goodbye to his mother, sister, and father, but Dovid shocked him by saying, "If you can wait until ten o'clock, I will go with you." Levi looked puzzled. He wanted to ask "why," but did not dare. Instead, he just smiled and told his father, "That would be great." Dovid looked at Batel with a smile, searching for agreement. Batel nodded, and then Dovid said, "Good, then it is settled. At ten we will leave." Upon their arrival in Bethsaida, they realized that the town was abuzz with the knowledge that Jesus was alive. The stories of His resurrection had already reached the entire region of Galilee. Many people were singing praises and praying, for this town was a place where Jesus spent much of His time. Many of the disciples came from this fishing town, and its inhabitants were very excited about the news.

Dovid could not understand all the excitement. When Levi began talking to people, inquiring whether they had seen the men who were with Jesus, the people informed him that they had gone up to Mount Tabor to meet with the Lord. Levi realized that he and his father had just passed through that area. They told him not to worry, that they would be back before dusk. They invited Levi and Dovid to stay with them for the evening. Dovid politely said, "Thank you, but we must get back home." He explained that since they had been gone for so long, he had to get back to work. One of the men Levi and his father were talking to was so excited about telling them all the things that the Lord had done. Dovid asked the man, "How do you *know* Jesus has done these things all over this region?" Now serious and with a stern look, the man looked at Dovid and testified, "A year ago, I could not look you in the eye because I was blind. The Lord restored my sight. Ask anyone in this town. They will tell you I was born blind and did not see until the Lord healed me. The Lord has accomplished many miracles here and all around this area. Blessed is the Lord of His people." Dovid was surprised by what he had just heard. Levi looked down, not wanting to look at his father for fear that he might smile and anger him. They met person after person who were all praising Jesus. Levi told the man, "We will wait a little while and hope they come. If not, may I please stay with you, for my father must return this evening?" "Yes, by all means! My home is open to you." Dovid cannot help but think, "Can all these people be false witnesses?"

As the hour was approaching about four in the afternoon, they heard loud voices coming from the main road, and a crowd was gathering. Levi recognized some of the men that he saw in the distance. He told his father, "It is the disciples. Let us go out to meet them." Dovid replied, "I will stay right here. You go ahead." So Levi went out to greet them. They were talking about what they had seen and the greatness of the Lord. Levi noticed that Peter was doing most of the talking. He could see clearly that John stayed quietly in the background, so Levi went over and greeted him. John smiled, and Levi told him that he had been anxiously waiting to see him and the others to find out what happened. John went on to tell him that so much had happened that there was not enough time to tell him everything. Dovid, watching from a distance, felt small and no longer needed in his son's life.

Levi was so excited. He was looking behind John, and John asked him, "For whom are you looking?" Levi replied, "Jesus. Is He here?" John told him, "No, we were with Him on the mountain, but He is gone." "When will you see Him again?" John replied, "I do not know." Then a voice from behind him said, "So where did He go?" Levi spun around quickly to see Dovid. "My apologies, I am Dovid from Scythopolis. Levi is my son." John shook his head, "Yes, I remember you. I met you the night they took the Lord." Dovid said, "Yes, that is correct." Dovid continued, "So you do not know where He is?" "No, I am sorry I do not, but He appeared to us, and then He was gone." "Is He a ghost or some kind of spirit?" "Oh no, He is real! We have touched Him. He has eaten with us, but He is God, so the Lord can come and go as He wishes." Dovid asked, "Well, if He is God, why does He not show Himself to us so that we can all see Him and believe?" John was about to answer when a man from behind him placed his arm on Dovid's shoulder and said in a loud voice so that everyone could hear, "The

Lord Jesus Christ has been seen by us all, and He will reveal Himself to those He wishes. My brother, you must walk in faith, for while He was with us, He told us that He would suffer many things for our sins and then would die at the hands of His people; yet, He would be raised up again. God has kept His promises to us from the beginning, and He has sent us the Messiah, but many have chosen not to accept Him." Dovid leaned over and whispered in Levi's ear, "Who is this man speaking?" Levi tells him that the man is Peter whom he had also met that night. Dovid now shook his head affirmatively. Peter continued to tell the crowd, "Our Lord has risen, and He goes to be with the Father. Know now that you must repent of your sins. Ask Jesus to intercede with the Father on your behalf as He is the way to the Father. For He has told us that, if you have seen Him, you have seen the *Father*!

Dovid, now frightened speaks, "How can this be? If you have seen *Him*, you have seen the *Father?*" He looked at Levi and said, "This makes no sense. I must return home. Levi, are you coming with me?" The feeling of stress and anxiety returned to Levi as he looked at his father and said, "I wish to stay here. I will be home in a day or so, if you do not mind." Dovid replied, "That will be fine. I do not understand who would believe this nonsense. If God raised Him from the dead, why will He not show Himself to the world?" Levi looked at his father and said, "You must have faith and know that with God all things are possible."

Dovid backed away from his son and turned to head home. Levi watched his father walk away and thought, "He refuses to accept what is truth." Levi watched him until he could no longer see him. He then turned around to walk back to the group. The former blind man could see that Levi was struggling with his faith and knowing the right thing to do. He put his arm around Levi and said, "Son, I can see your faith is being tested. I tell you that God healed me through

Jesus Christ our Lord, and He has done the same for many others here and all over this area. I tell you this, search the Scriptures and see that it was foretold of His good deeds in healing the blind, the sick, and the lame. Trust in Him who was sent to save the world, and know that He is with you always!" Levi agreed with him and said, "I have; I am just struggling because my family does not also accept Him." "The Lord will find a way to heal all of us," the man told Levi.

On that day, all the people who heard what Peter and the other disciples said, were saved and came to know Jesus as their Lord and Savior. Levi spent the next few days with the disciples and the other people who knew Jesus and had witnessed His ministry. He learned more and was baptized in the Holy Spirit by one of the disciples. The disciples went out from there, back to Jerusalem, but stopped on the way and spent time with Levi's family, along with Azel and his family. Many in Scythopolis were also saved. Dovid continued to fight his feelings about what others felt was correct. As they were leaving for Jerusalem, Dovid told Levi, "I do not believe what I cannot see." Levi said to his father, "How do you know that God is real then?" No response was forthcoming. Levi felt sad for his father because he refused to see what was in front of him. Levi bade his mother and family farewell and headed back to Jerusalem with the disciples.

JESUS SEEN BY THE MASSES

✝

Crowds were now following the disciples, and as they got back to Jerusalem, it came to pass that Levi and many of Jesus' followers were gathered together, meeting and sharing the good news with everyone. Jesus stood among them, spoke to them, and said, "Peace be with you!" The total number of people was about five hundred. He spoke to them and told them to be of good cheer, and assured the people that He would be with them until the end of time. As He spoke to them, Levi could not help but look at the ground in fear of being in the presence of the Lord God. What an incredible honor to be in His very presence! Levi was filled with such awe that, even with his eyes closed he could still see Jesus' face and could not help but notice how white His garments were. His whole body was bright and shining. Just as quickly as He appeared, He was gone. When the people rose again to discuss what He had told them, they were so excited that they were talking over one another making it impossible to understand what each person saw and heard. Interestingly enough, others who heard of this meeting maintained that their tales were all a fabrication—just as before—merely a made-up story.

Over the next several weeks, the disciples reported that they were with Jesus many times, and that He had told them that He was going away and that He was sending them a helper who would guide them and give them the power to spread the Gospel. *He commanded them to go and bear witness of Him in Jerusalem, and in Judea and Samaria, and to the ends of the earth.*

Levi was blessed to befriend all the disciples, and when they returned to Jerusalem, they were instructed to go into the upper room; all of them, including Mary, His mother, His brothers, and the other Mary, along with the faithful, numbering about one-hundred and twenty. They all prayed in one accord and with supplication until the day of Pentecost had arrived fully. *Then the Holy Spirit came with wind and fire and divided tongues of fire, and one sat upon each of them. They were all filled with the Holy Spirit and began to speak in other tongues as the Spirit gave them utterance.* Levi thought, "This day is the same day in our heritage that the LORD gave us the Torah. Today, we again receive the Word of God."

Levi later returned to Scythopolis. When he got home, he immediately began to preach the Gospel of Jesus Christ and the Resurrection. Many people in the town and the nearby towns were saved and baptized by Levi and the other Apostles. Azel helped Levi set up a church in his hometown, and helped him lead others to Christ. They went out to preach the Good News to the world. When the town fell on hard times, Batel began to help Levi feed the poor and clothe the naked, and she helped set up a school for the young children of those families who were believers. She became a believer just a few years later, along with Levi's sister Eidel. At the age of fourteen, Eidel was baptized. The only member of the family who remained true to his traditional beliefs was Dovid. Levi conducted long conversations with his father, but he always disagreed. When Batel became a believer, he blamed it on Levi and stopped talking to his son for awhile. Dovid was angry, and they did not even see each other for about three years. Every chance Dovid got, he avoided his son. If Levi came over to spend time with his mother or sister, Dovid made a point to be gone by the time he arrived. Even when Levi married and had children, Dovid was not present. Eventually, Dovid developed into a bitter old man. Ten years had gone by, and Levi was now a full Apostle of the Lord, working in the community and outside the town in which he lived.

BATEL BECOMES ILL

✟

It had come to pass that Batel became very ill, and Dovid realized how grave the situation was. He went to the synagogue daily to pray that God would heal his wife. He asked God to punish him and take him, but to leave his wife. He prayed and prayed, but the more he did, the worse she became. Levi was now at her bedside, along with his sister, her husband, their children, and Levi's wife and two children. They were praying, and Levi was talking to his mother about heaven and what Jesus had done for her. He spoke of how she should no longer fear death, that with Jesus one would not die but have eternal life and that His death and resurrection has paid the debt for their sins. He reminded Batel that Jesus had promised that she would be with Him in heaven by her acceptance of the Lord as her personal Lord and Savior. Dovid was in the background listening to his son and the words he was using.

For the first time, Dovid's heart was open, mostly because he was exhausted from all the pain and worry of Batel's illness. Levi did not realize that Dovid was behind him. He told his mother, "I know that the Lord will keep you, and that He is faithful to those who love Him." Dovid listened intently as Levi spoke of heaven and what the Lord had told them what heaven was going to be like. Then Dovid broke down and began to sob. Levi turned around and saw his father whom he had not seen in quite some time. He was old, gray, fragile, and hunched-over. Levi turned and got up to leave so that Dovid could have some time alone with Batel. Dovid looked at Levi. As Levi walked past him, Dovid grabbed his hand and pleaded, "Do not go! Please continue. I desire to hear more." Levi turned around and looked at his mother, who smiled through her pain. Batel whispered, "I have been given a great gift. I have gotten to see my husband and my son together again before I die. God has answered my prayers." Levi looked at his father, as Dovid moved closer to her bed. He knelt by her side and said, "I love you. I am so sorry I did not give you more in your life." She shook her head, "You have nothing to be sorry about, for you have loved me and given me a great life."

By this time, the whole family was crying, and Levi could see that his mother was fading, so he told them all to hold hands and pray. He prayed, "Lord, would you look over your child and would you grant our mother peace in heaven with all those who have gone before her." He asked, "God would you heal our family and protect us." He further prayed, "Father, would you please send the Holy Spirit to comfort our family during this difficult time. Amen." As he finished his prayer, he opened his eyes and witnessed his mother take her last breath.

The entire family now surrounded her bed, weeping for their loss. Levi told them, "Fear not for the Lord will protect her and keep her. For God sent us His Son to take our place on that Cross, and because of this unselfish act, we have been forgiven our sins." Dovid looked at Levi, but did not understand what he was speaking about. This was not the time to question what was said. Levi then read from the Psalms of David: *"The Lord is my light and my salvation; whom shall I fear? The Lord is the strength of my life. Though an*

army may encamp against me, my heart shall not fear," and,
*"One thing I have desired of the Lord; that will I seek: That
I may dwell in the house of the Lord all the days of my life."*
Levi finished, "We request these things to be granted upon us
through your Son Jesus Christ our Lord! Amen."

A few days later, Levi was finalizing things at his parent's
home, and preparing to take his family back to their home,
just outside of town. Levi now traveled frequently. Most of
his time was spent in Gesers, a city that had experienced
tremendous growth during this period. It was the area where
Jesus had cleansed a man with unclean spirits. Plenty of
work was left for Levi to do there, as well as in many of
the small villages nearby. Because of Levi's message, he
had seen many people come to know the Lord. Azel and his
whole family had become the leaders of the local church in
Scythopolis. Word of Azel's work was reaching Jerusalem,
mostly because of Levi writing to the disciples who, in turn
wrote to tell Azel how proud they were of the work he was
doing in Christ's name.

DOVID SEEKS GUIDANCE

✝

Dovid stopped his son and requested, "Do you have a minute so that I can ask you a few questions?" Levi said, "Of course, Father." Dovid was now years older, and all the anger and bitterness had been replaced with reflection and regret for what had happened since he separated from his son.

"Levi, I desire to hear more about your ministry." Dovid was now asking as a proud father, no longer wanting to disprove his son's beliefs, so Levi discussed his mission and told his father how many souls were coming to the Lord. Dovid listened to Levi as he thought to himself that he, as the father, was no longer the teacher, but the student. Ironically, Levi wanted to make certain that he understood what had happened over the last several years. He no longer was angry with his father for the separation that caused his family to be absent when he married or when his children were born. He had come to the realization that forgiveness was imperative if he was to truly practice what the Lord had taught.

Dovid told Levi, "I have heard of the thousands of people who have come to accept Jesus, and I have also heard that many of your fellow Priests...." Levi interrupted and interjected, "We are called Apostles." "I am sorry; Apostles are being killed for what you believe. Is that true?" "Yes, Father. It is; however, what we believe and what we know does not come from ourselves. It comes from God through His Son, Jesus Christ, and is given to us through the Holy Spirit." "Levi, I have tried to understand your thinking, and I have prayed for understanding that I may know what you know and accept what you believe, but it has been hard for me to do so. What you must understand is that all I know is the laws and the traditions given to us from Moses so many years ago. I do not know any other way."

"Father, Jesus has told us that He is the way, the truth, and the life, and that no one can go to the Father unless it is through Him." "But why, Levi? Why?" "What I have come to know is that God needed to find a way to bring us back into a relationship with Him. We are a sinful nation, and since God cannot look upon our sins, He sent His Son to pay the price for those sins. We may now go before the throne of God, because of the work His Son did on the Cross. Jesus paid the price for us! We are free, and as long as we accept Jesus as our Lord and Savior, we can enter freely into the Kingdom of Heaven."

Dovid told Levi, "Yes, I know about the cross. I saw Him there." Levi looked puzzled, "What do you mean you saw Him there?" "I was there. I went and saw what they did to Him. I looked on from a distance." "Why did you not ever tell me this?" "Because I felt you were too young to understand. It was the worst experience I have ever had. I will never forget the look on His face and of everyone else who was a witness as they hung Him there. The thing I do not understand is that He was praying to God to forgive them for what they did. He said, 'they do not know what they are doing.' I did not understand that." "I do," Levi continued. "You see, Jesus came to save all of us, not just a select few, and He would have forgiven even those who did what they did to Him if they had accepted Him as the Lord." "Levi,

how can it be that easy?" "Because we have all fallen short
of the glory of God, and nothing we do—no matter how
great—can ever be enough to get us into heaven. We must
see that Jesus is the only way. He is the light unto my path.
He is the resurrection, and God has granted all things unto
Him on earth as it is in heaven."

Dovid then asked Levi, "So what does one have to do to be
accepted then?" "You must ask for forgiveness of your sins,
and ask Jesus to come into your life and be your Lord and
Savior. That is it." Dovid, truly puzzled, questioned, "That is
all I have to do—what about following the commandments?
What about our traditions?" "Yes Father, you should do good
deeds, but they alone are not enough. Come let me pray with
you this prayer so that you can accept Jesus for who He is
and be able to see Mother again someday in heaven." "Wait
Levi, what about all those who say He is a fake; that Jesus
of Nazareth died and did not rise again?" "Father, you told
me you saw Him on that cross. Was He dead?" "Yes! Of
course, there was no doubt about that!" "Well, I have seen
Him myself since then, alive and well—not in a dream or a
vision, but in an actual physical being." "When was that?"
"I was with the disciples and about five hundred others when
Jesus Christ appeared to us and spoke to us about the truth,
and about the things to come." "Levi, what about all those I
heard are being persecuted by the Pharisees? Some followers
are being beaten and killed. Tell me, are you not worried
about what will become of all the believers?" "No. I know
God, and I know that Jesus told us that if we are persecuted
and called names because of Him, we will be called *blessed*.
He also told us that whatever we ask, if we ask it in His
name, it will be granted to us by the Father."

"Father, do you remember a man named Saul of Tarsus?"
He was one of the most powerful Pharisees Dovid knew. In
fact, Saul of Tarsus was being groomed to be High Priest
some day. "Yes, I remember, and he was notorious for being

the biggest persecutor of the followers of Jesus." "Did you hear that he had become a follower as well?" "What? I cannot believe it; he was vehemently against Jesus' ministry." "Well, he encountered Jesus on the road one day, and his whole life has changed. Once the chief persecutor, he is now a great Apostle sharing the Gospel with the entire world. He went from the hunter to the hunted. He is now responsible for thousands coming to know the Lord." "Impossible Levi! He was a zealot for the laws and traditions of our people." "Yes Father, I know. Do you think that a man who knows the law better than anyone else would change everything, his power and his privileges and put his own life in danger for a fake?" "It is hard to imagine that he would." "Father, any of the men I have spoken about, as well as those who have died, have gone willingly to their death without denying that Jesus Christ is the Lord."

Levi pleaded, "Father, please accept Jesus Christ and enjoy eternity in heaven with all the saints and your family." At this, Dovid became so upset and began to cry. Levi asked his father, "What is it that you wish you had Father? What is the one thing for which you long?" Dovid responded, "I wish to have peace in my heart and I long for truth." "Then allow Jesus to come into your life and receive the truth and experience peace that will last for eternity."

Still weeping, Dovid fell on the floor, and Levi brought him up to his knees and put his hand on his father's shoulder and prayed for him. Then he asked Dovid to pray for the forgiveness of his sins, and asked Jesus to come into his life. After Dovid did this, Levi said, "Father, welcome into the Kingdom of God. You are now a child of God!" Dovid looked up at his son and realized that Levi had also been crying. He was emotionally overwhelmed with what had just occurred. Eidel was behind them and came over and put her arms around her father and held him tight. They were all now weeping, but this time, weeping tears of joy and thankfulness for what God had done.

DOVID'S EYES OPENED TO THE TRUTH

✝

Dovid then told Levi, "I have been so foolish, all this wasted time. I have allowed my pride and stubbornness to rule my decisions. I lost my son and myself in the process. I am so unworthy of this blessing, and I am ashamed of who I have become." Levi stopped his father and said, "The good news is that you are a new creation in Christ, and from this day forward you start anew. That is the Good News of the Gospel—that God sent His Son so that you would be forgiven your sins, and that you will have eternity with the Lord in Heaven."

Dovid now realized that all Levi had said was true. Levi told his father, "You see, all that time I spent working on the Scriptures was important. It brought me to this place. God used my understanding of the law to help me preach to all those, like you, who know the law, but who cannot make the bridge to who Jesus is." Dovid, now proud of what had happened, replied, "I feel such incredible relief. Somehow the entire weight that has been on my shoulders has vanished. I only wish that your mother was here to see it. You know, she told me I was an old fool, and I should open my heart to hear God's Word, but I would not pay attention to her."

Levi, I have one final question, "Why does God want to save me? I am no one. I have nothing to give in return. Why would He care about saving me? At least you are a man of God who understands His Word and works, but me—I am nothing!" "Father, God loves all His children, and He cares deeply for each and every one of us, but the LORD does give us free will to either accept or reject Him. Those who do accept Him will have rewards in Heaven. You see Father, Jesus took your place on that cross. If God were to condemn all that were deserving of that punishment, crosses would line the world from one end to the other. For we all deserve His punishment, yet He took that punishment upon Himself so that we might be forgiven. His grace and mercy is abundant for His children and those who believe in His Son. How blessed are we that have the LORD—the Father of all creation—as our God?"

"Levi, I thought that I had lost everything, and I prayed many nights that God would help me to forgive and forget, but I just did not see it or understand it. God has opened my eyes to the truth, and I realize that the prayer I made all those years ago, as we made the pilgrimage from our home here to the Holy City, has come true." Levi asked, "What do you mean?" "I prayed that we would be blessed by the Passover and that God would help make our family strong and successful. I also prayed that God would give you the wisdom to be a good leader and Rabbi and/or Pharisee. He has granted our family many things. We are no longer separated by the disagreement of what we believe. Our family is back together, and you have become one of the most powerful leaders in our area, an Apostle for Jesus Christ, our Lord of all nations." Levi smiled and said, "Yes Father, we have been blessed. So has the entire world. God has done great things in our generation and for all those who will come after us!"

As they prepared for the evening meal, the entire family gathered around the table with Dovid. Levi prayed over the meal and gave thanks to God for the food, and the blessings of reuniting his family. He prayed for all those in the world who still did not know Jesus, and asked that they would come to know Him and His Glory; that no one would ever be separated by the cross again!

AUTHOR'S AFTERWORD

✝

This story depicts the experience of a family that has a strong understanding of God and His mercy. Yet, through it all, only one member saw His grace and love through His Son Jesus Christ.

How is it that one can see what others do not? From the beginning, Levi understood who Jesus was—not because of the deeds He performed, as much as by His speaking the Word. I took some of the text out of the NKJV and utilized some details from the internet. Many of us have read the accounts of what Jesus did and what He said, so eloquently written in the four Gospels. Yet, these stories are shaped and formed, mostly by those who traveled with Him and were around our Lord. I wanted to weave the story from a different point of view—that of a young man of just thirteen. If you examine this story about Levi's family, it parallels Jesus' parable of the sower.

> *"Behold, a sower went out to sow. And as he sowed, some seed fell by the wayside and the birds came and devoured them. Some fell on stony places, where they did not have much earth; and they immediately sprang up because they had no depth of earth.*

But when the sun was up they were scorched, and because they had no root they withered away. And some fell among thorns, and the thorns sprang up and choked them. But others fell on good ground and yielded a crop; some a hundredfold, some sixty, some thirty. He, who has ears to hear, let him hear!" (Luke 8:4-8)

Clearly, the seed in this parable is the Word of God. Like many in those days, of the words that Jesus spoke, some fell by the wayside, meaning that many of the people did not understand what He was saying. Others received the Word, but once things got a little difficult and they were asked to commit to what they believed, they backed off and changed their minds. Still others, much like Dovid, heard the Word and understood what was being said, but because they were so caught up in what was important to them, they immediately dropped it for worldly things such as traditions and the laws. Finally, there was Levi and Azel and the many, many others who heard the Word of God and believed. The Word was planted firmly in their hearts, and they did not waiver, no matter what.

I tried to show the importance of not only knowing God's Word, but staying strong and maintaining one's faith. In those times, it was very difficult to do this; yes, they saw Jesus and saw the things He did. If they saw Him raise Lazarus from the dead, why would they not believe? That is a difficult question to answer. More importantly, they saw and believed for a while, but still turned their heads and walked away.

The seed was sown, yet the ground was not of good soil, but praise God for His mercy and fulfilling His promises to send someone who would atone for the sins of all mankind. That is why He sent His Son and in so doing, Jesus tended the soil. Even today, the soil can be worked and enriched so that when the right person comes along and sows a new seed, it can take root and be strong. Levi did this, not only for his whole family, but for so many others as well.

While Levi and his family were separated by the cross for many years, it was his father who created the situation whereby causing a split between Levi and the rest of his family. Yet, Levi never lost his faith. Even though the reunion occurred at the end of this story, in real life that is not always the case. In reality, Jesus' death on that cross was the dividing line between God and all the people who did not believe in His Son. It remains so even today. When Levi was separated by his beliefs, he had the choice to drop what he knew to be right and follow Jesus Christ or to accept the worldly view. He, like many others, chose to pick up his cross and follow Jesus. The truth is that even today, many families, all over the world are separated by this decision. Some are carrying the burden for their whole families and have been set apart or alienated by what they believe. I heard a man from India preach in our church one day. He told us that he was interested in the Gospel and began to read about this man named Jesus and came to accept Jesus Christ as his Lord and Savior. He was not only kicked out of his home, but was threatened with death in his village. His life was truly in jeopardy. So, not everyone has the chance to reunite with their family. This is a very sensitive subject for most people. Unfortunately many people would rather not discuss their beliefs, because they would have to explain why they feel the way they do. Since most cannot express why they feel the way they do, they just do not say anything. In the book, Levi was determined to do what he believed was his calling. As it turned out in the end, the person who was really separated was Dovid. All of Levi's family had come to believe in Jesus Christ, accepted Him, and were baptized. Dovid realized that what they had was peace of mind, fulfillment, and love. Dovid recognized that he lacked all of that and basically was isolated at the end of this life; however, once he accepted what he had fought all his life, he was freed.

I wanted to show that in Levi's life, the key factor was that he never gave up on what he knew was right. In the end, he brought his whole family to Christ!

Today is no different. We all know people who need the love of Jesus Christ, yet we sometimes are fearful to discuss it. We do not want them to be upset with us or stop talking to us. We fear the rejection of the friendship or the loved one, so we do not discuss it, because we want to stay connected to them. Yet, we are causing a much greater separation, because they will be separated from us in eternity. Do you sometimes feel this way also? Today is a great day to change, like Levi who told Dovid, his father, "Today everything is new!" We have the chance to bring those who are separated from God into a relationship with Him through His Son. No greater feeling exists than knowing that you have your eternity secured through His blood.

Do not allow the world to dictate your beliefs; do not let the materialistic things of the world be what you, and those you love, find most important in life. If you are fearful of what will happen, allowing them to know your true feelings is okay. Trust in the Lord, and He will give you strength.

That is what Levi did. He continued to sow the seed God had given him to sow. Sometimes the harvest takes longer to be gathered, but if you tend and water it every day, sooner or later, it will grow strong and beautiful, and it will last for all eternity. This is what happened to this family through the one person, Levi, who understood God's Word.

Notice also that Levi left the door open for his father to accept Jesus as his Lord and Savior, and by doing that, his father realized it was not too late. Jesus tells us the same thing—it is never too late to accept Him. No matter what you have done, no matter what you have said, no matter what you should have done, He still loves you. Even if you have left Him, He wants you back. He loves you, He always has, and He always will. *"No greater love is there than this."* The only time it will be too late is the day you die, but do not wait for that day. Come home and accept the Lord, for He is waiting for you. Call upon His name and accept Him for who He is, and all your sins will be wiped away. Levi knew this, and finally so did Dovid. Having accepted Him, the Lord has wiped away all his sins and he started anew.

My prayer is that if you know someone who does not know and accept Jesus, that you will share the Gospel with them. For those who read this book and do not know that the blood of Christ has covered your sins, I would encourage you to read the four Gospels of Matthew, Mark, Luke and John, and ask questions of friends and family who have a relationship with Jesus. Then you will know for yourself whether or not He is who He claimed to be.

My hope is that all my brothers and sisters would come to know Jesus Christ personally and begin a relationship with Him.